AB TERRA 2024

AB TERRA 2024

EDITED BY YEN OOI · AND · DAWN OSTLUND

Cover design by Dawn Ostlund.

Published in the United States by Ab Terra Books, an imprint of Brain Mill Press.

Print ISBN 978-1-948559-96-6

EPUB ISBN 978-1-948559-97-3

CONTENTS

TO START, LET'S PUT THE SCIENCE IN SCIENCE FICTION AND DO A SMALL (THOUGHT) EXPERIMENT. WHEN YOU REACH THE END OF THIS SENTENCE, PLEASE CLOSE your eyes and think of the moon.

Done thinking? What did you imagine? The image of a moon waxing, waning, new, or full? A crescent sharp as a scythe? A lunar face composed of craters and shadows? Maybe you thought of the concept of a moon rather than an image; maybe you remembered a time you went stargazing, or a night when the moonlight was bright enough to see by; maybe you heard the tune of a song like "Moondance" or "Fly Me to the Moon."

The point of this thought experiment is that no two readers of this anthology will imagine the same thing. Each person will approach the question in different ways, informed by different experiences, biases, and backgrounds. (Even the orientation of the moon as viewed from Earth is determined by latitude—the same moon will look quite different when viewed from the equator as opposed to further north or south.) You have your moon; the next reader has theirs. And just as no two people will imagine the same moon, no two experiences of the stories in this anthology will be exactly alike.

In fact, this is one of my favorite aspects of fiction: how stories exist as a dialogue between reader and author, creating in real time a reading experience uniquely informed by both parties. In science fiction, this often manifests through shared curiosity. Authors grapple with ideas (some weird, some wonderful, some new, some old) about how the world works or how it might work someday—and use those ideas to turn a mirror on humanity. The backgrounds and expectations readers bring into this conversation, in turn, contribute to the richness of a story. Combine a diversity of readers with a diversity of authors, and you get a vibrant space for entertainment, philosophy, theorizing, and more.

(Because sci-fi is *fun*. It's *cool*. And sometimes it hits you with concepts that make your head spin: either alongside the fun/cool parts, or seeded so neatly within them that the big ideas take you by surprise.)

There's another aspect to the moon analogy. Every person will imagine their own moon; on the flip side, the moon itself is still shared, a universal referent for us Earthlings. Even as our concepts of it diverge, the thing itself unites us. Science fiction is ours, too, tying us together even as we take different things from it. And if you've ever reread an influential story years later only to have an entirely different response, you'll know that stories can, across time, even tie *you* to different versions of yourself.

Perhaps a decade from now the same thing will happen with an *Ab Terra* story. After all, *Ab Terra* is a space for those fun, cool, and mind-bending sci-fi ideas mentioned earlier—and a sense of discovery through fiction has been baked into this anthology series from the beginning. We've been speaking of our perspective on the moon from Earth; how about the view of Earth from the moon, a spectacular sight first seen by human eyes as recently as the 1960s? The wonder conjured by "Earthrise" serves as inspiration for *Ab Terra*. This series seeks to encapsulate that rare and remarkable feeling of a total perspective shift on a familiar world.

I used the moon in the earlier thought experiment for one more reason: science fiction has long been preoccupied with celestial bodies, and the stories in this year's *Ab Terra* are no different. Moons, stars, and far-off planets—sometimes familiar, sometimes beyond our current knowledge—populate this year's crop of stories. From a jaded moon dust expert to a grieving lunar colonist; from a generation ship physicist on his way to a new home planet to a groundbreaking astronaut forever looking towards her old one, the main characters in many of these stories reckon with their relationship to their past—and their Earth—in myriad ways.

It's not just the stories set in space that ask the big questions. One story addresses the relationship between two mothers with foreknowledge of their children's shared future here on Earth, while another posits the (un)reality of an artificial "mirror-verse" could be preferred to our own. Two pieces feature robots—drastically different from each other—questioning everything they've been taught, playing with very human ideas from a non-human perspective. In short, an eclectic assortment of carefully curated sci-fi awaits you in the following pages.

So, time to imagine one last thing. Imagine you're about to read an anthology filled with a diversity of authors ready to share their short story worlds with you. Each story you read will welcome you to a unique conversation, made possible only by your interaction with it. You're creating your experience of the story just as much as the words on the page. It is your moon; these are your stories.

Are you ready? Welcome to *Ab Terra*. I hope you enjoy the ride.

Tia Tashiro

AB TERRA 2024

YOU WILL LET ME BE

- BY JOHN BRADY

The glossy investor prospectus, a few copies of which could still be found in the back office, boasted that the Sparkly Promised Future Clinic LLC provided "best-on-the-planet" life-downtime care to super-high-net-worth individuals determined to discontinue the cycle of life's turning. And when it looked like the technology to reanimate cryogenically frozen bodies and/or download previously digitized consciousnesses into new, bespoke cultured physiques was really, truly right around the corner, the clinic did big business, the desire of certain people to establish their mastery over death providing customers by the bucketful.

Yet when the nearness of that corner turned out to be a mirage that sat stubbornly shimmering on the horizon no matter how many hopeful steps were taken toward it, the clinic, along with many of its sister establishments—low-end to high-end—

was mothballed. The reanimation professionals were disappointed. The investors wrote down their losses and licked their wounds. The patients, luckily oblivious, could not, either by contract or by law, be abandoned. Thus, they were maintained in suspended animation. Frozen. Siliconized. Waiting. Probably forever. But maybe not. Hopefully not?

Though not everyone was disappointed. As with many situations in the affairs of humankind, there were some sharp and clever people who, lacking scruples or, more generously, having differently calibrated scruples, managed to mine the silver lining these clouds.

o

"HURRY UP!" SLIM SAID.

Lying under the cryo-bed on the cold concrete floor, Bennie thought briefly of stabbing Slim in the leg with his screwdriver. What the fuck did he think Bennie was doing, taking a nap? Admiring the bed's sleek, gently curved underside obviously chosen by the clinic's designers to convey a thinned, hygienic futurism? Bennie didn't stab Slim. He did briefly think of asking him why he called himself or allowed himself to be called Slim. He wasn't obviously skinny. He also wasn't grossly overweight. So there was no physical reason—nonironic or ironic—why he should be called Slim. Did it have to do with where he grew up? Maybe out West among cowboy folk with similar nicknames like Tex or Doc or Old Fast Hands? But then you would think he would wear cowboy boots instead of the boots he did wear—army surplus ones from the Third War of the Desert. Worth finding out about? No, not at that moment. So Bennie didn't do that either. Instead, he concentrated on the task at hand, quickly grunting an "I'm going as fast as I can."

He was, too. It wasn't his fault that the neural link portal had corroded and he couldn't patch in. He chipped at the portal with his screwdriver, and crystals of what looked like glittering rusty salts flaked off. "The portal's messed up," he reported between picks. "I have to clean it. Long time since anybody did any maintenance in here."

"Uh-huh. Sure," Slim replied. "Doesn't mean someone won't show up to catch us. So hurry up, like I said."

Yeah, that fucker's getting stabbed, Bennie thought. *Not now. But at some point.*

°

NO ONE THINKS, *I'm gonna grow up and be a picker.* Just like probably no one used to think, *I'm gonna grow up and be a garbage man.* Bennie thought the comparison particularly apt. Although not because the jobs were the same. Garbage men had picked up garbage. Pickers picked over the lives of others. The garbage guys collected stuff nobody wanted and that often smelled or was rotting. Pickers collected something different. If there was a body, it almost never smelled. Those things were really well-preserved. Digitally preserved minds didn't smell, of course. Bytes have no odor. People would be justified in making that comparison and drawing that conclusion because the jobs were both of low status. Which wasn't to say that they sucked objectively. Only that people thought they sucked. Subjectively. And that had power to influence behavior, including what people thought or didn't think about another person's line of work. That's why it would make sense to draw that parallel. You could try and divert attention from the reality of your career's perceived undesirability by saying you were a sanitation worker or, as Bennie did, a biographical archivist and data retriever. In either case, it wasn't a very effective tactic. People saw through the bullshit. Then they still wouldn't think much of you. Maybe they thought even less of you because of your chickenshit move to try and disguise the reality of your situation. People didn't respect the garbage man because of the trash and the smelling part. They didn't respect a picker because it was illegal and kinda creepy. And in the end, they didn't respect you more because you tried to lie about it.

o

BACK AT THE FIRM AFTER HIS AND SLIM'S HEIST, Bennie sat at his work station fiddling with his scanner.

"You in yet?"

Bennie's boss, Earl, was asking. That wasn't a nickname. It was his real, if somewhat old-fashioned, name. Although if anyone in the firm deserved a nickname, it was him. Bennie thought this because Earl had a pronounced personality trait. The sort of readily identifiable trait that could deservedly attract a nickname like a magnet pulling in iron filings. Earl had the shortest of short fuses. He could and did fly off the handle at disruptions both large and small to what he perceived to be the current plan. He would get crazy mad. Very fast. Very strongly. Psychotically, irrationally angry. Creamy white spittle collecting at the corners of his lips mad. *Psycho* would have been an obvious choice. Or if you wanted to be like the mob guys in the classic movies Bennie watched to try to fall asleep, something like "Earl Eight Fits" would have worked, too.

Then, yeah, it was a bit of a risk for Bennie to answer Earl's question with a casual, "Not yet, what's the rush?"

Although not that much of a risk, because the answer was so obvious that Earl would know Bennie was kidding. Had to be kidding, because the guy they were picking was an absolute whale. If—no, *when* they cracked him, they could live off the payday for a year. At least.

But just in case he didn't know, Bennie quickly added, "Almost, boss. Almost in."

Earl clapped him on the shoulder. Hard. Though not about to explode with rage hard. More just being a leader trying to motivate the troops hard. "Good. Tell me as soon as you're in."

Ah, the mellowing effect of fantasies of future riches, Bennie thought to himself. As he turned back to the screen, he smiled and continued with his work.

Although it wasn't the work of getting in. That was already done—soon after Bennie had loaded the guy into the scanner and started cruising around his consciousness. Which was strange, because rich dudes who had themselves frozen or their minds written into silicone with the expectation of future revival or injection planned ahead. Hoping to continue their rich-dude habits of amassing even more riches once they were woken up, they squirreled away sizable nuts to kickstart their ascent back to the level of luxury to which they had accustomed themselves before death's first visit. They didn't want pickers like Bennie messing around in their minds trying to find their treasure, and they protected themselves. This guy? Not so much, seemingly. There was nothing. No passwords. No firewalls. No false, digitally constructed memories to throw him off the scent. Just a vast field of thoughts as far as one could see.

Rows and rows of days. One after the other. Ready to be picked.

Bennie adjusted the scanner's resolution. He pulled back on the stick to a comfortable cruising altitude. First, get a lay of the land. The peaks and valleys of this guy's life. Highs and lows. Degrees. Marriages. Births of children. Affairs. First million. First billion. First trillion. Stuff like that. Nothing particular. Because the particular was messy with details, and details could be dangerous. They aroused emotions. Start grubbing around in the day-to-day life of a guy you're planning to pick, and suddenly you find yourself engrossed by an up-from-tragedy story, one that starts with the guy being abused as a kid at the hand of an alcoholic father particularly adept at making his son feel worthless but ultimately turns, as the guy overcomes the wounds—both physical and psychological—to become a titan of industry. And not just any titan. An enlightened one. A boss who treated his workers more or less well and was also a steward of the community, giving plenty to charity and advocating for generally the right causes. A guy who *this* present time could use. Who'd be an addition. And who were you against this guy? You were a picker. A picker who was going to rob this guy blind and fuck up his resurrection even as you hid your tears and sniffles of sympathy. What a piece of shit you were. Nope. Nothing particular at first. That way? Only feelings and the pain of self-recrimination.

Dive too deep, too fast, and that's what you found. That's what was there.

So Bennie stayed up top in the metaphorical clouds. Making slow, lazy loops up and down the timeline. He scanned for the usual landmarks of privilege—private school education for the stiff and his kids, social and professional networks with other rich folks, a beautiful wife and more beautiful, younger lovers. Only after he had spotted enough to stoke his resentment and feed a sense that this guy had had his chance at the trough and didn't deserve to grub for more, a sense strong enough to inoculate Bennie against the subsequent discovery of any heartstring-pulling biographical details, did he descend closer. He scanned for an appropriate era. One with meaningful moments. The ones that became the ingredients blended into passwords and secret questions and other building blocks of security protocols. The kind of moments that a person would remember and more importantly would consider his own—uniquely his own. That he understood and knew in a way that no one else could know. No one else unless that no one was like Bennie, a rascally onlooker hovering there with access to everything.

Bennie decided to turn toward the guy's early midlife and the founding of the company that made him his coin. As good a time as any other, Bennie thought as he deployed the probe scripts. He watched them float down, steering with their spidery feelers open and hungry to explore.

And then they disappeared with a dazzling flash. Like meteorites burning up as they hit the atmosphere.

A voice asked, "Why are you doing this?"

Earl's hand clapped down on his shoulder. Harder this time. It also stayed there. "You in yet?"

The voice he'd heard on the scan—masculine but not hard and sharp like Earl's, softer and gentler—remained echoing in his ears, and he was slow to answer Earl.

No second clap on the shoulder. Earl just squeezed hard and asked the question again. Hissed it, really. "Are you in yet?"

"Yes. Yes," Bennie replied as the squeeze's pain followed gravity and nerves down his chest and back.

"And?" So much aggression packed into one three-letter word. If the pain wasn't focusing his attention elsewhere, Bennie would have taken more time to admire such densely packed hostility. Earl really was talented in that regard.

"And," Bennie continued, fighting to keep his voice steady, "I've completed the biographical scan and identified the periods most likely to yield the relevant exploitable data. I've released the first wave of probe scripts. They'll take some time to vacuum up the facts we'll need."

"Good," Earl said, and the hostility disappeared as quickly as it had appeared. *God, such a short fuse,* Bennie thought. The hand, however, stayed clamped down, and the pain continued its slip further down Bennie's torso. Then, just like that, Earl released his grip. Maybe it was the delirium of the pain, but Bennie could have sworn that Earl even gave his shoulder a tender, almost fatherly pat before continuing, "Anything strange in there? When I walked up, it looked like you had seen a ghost."

Bennie risked reigniting Earl's anger and turned to face him. "Strange? No, nothing strange at all. I was just concentrating, probably."

"Yeah, concentrating on trying not to fuck this up," Slim piped up from his workstation.

This time, Earl really did pat his shoulder. Then he turned and said definitively, "Shut the fuck up, Slim."

"Will do, boss," Slim replied without a pause, all the bravado leaking right out of his voice.

Bennie found himself pleased both at the rebuke and the thought of stabbing Slim at some point in the future. Because he was going to do it. Oh yes he was.

o

MUCH LATER THAT NIGHT, BENNIE SAT ON THE EDGE of his bed in his underwear. The blue glow from his phone mixed with his sallow skin. In that blend, Bennie looked pale green. He had been sitting there a long time, so long that he felt the first pricks of numbness where his butt compressed against his bed's fiberboard frame. Finally, he made up his mind and texted, **You up?**

That really wasn't the question. He knew she was up. This time—middle of the night—was when she liked to work.

No, the real question was whether she would answer. He pictured her at her desk in front of the screen, bathed in the same sort of digital glow lighting him. He saw her with her phone, looking at his message. If she snorted and laughed, there wouldn't be an answer. She'd put her phone screen-side down or maybe toss it on the bed behind her and get back to work, laughing and shaking her head one more time as the device hit the sheets. But if instead her usual work expression—determined and slightly exasperated—softened a little, and she paused to read the message one more time, well, then maybe, yes, she'd answer.

Eventually, Bennie turned his device off. He stretched out and tried to sleep. It took a while because the sound of her laugh kept echoing in his ears.

○

BENNIE OPENED THE WAREHOUSE DOOR, PUSHING its grooved wheel along the worn metal track. It screeched as he pushed, and in the early morning quiet it sounded like a murderous scream as it bounced off the other warehouses and echoed down the street. Bennie winced. He winced again when he pulled the door shut and it screeched again. Then he waved his discomfort away. He had something he wanted to test out, and he wanted to get to it.

He loaded the guy's mind in and started to cruise around. Avoiding yesterday's territory, he picked a time and let a set of probes fall. He watched them float down, silently counting down to when they would burn up and the spooky voice would announce itself. None of that happened. Instead, they landed without incident, and he watched as they got their bearings, deployed their feelers, and started looking for relevant biographical details, copying and storing the promising-looking ones.

Bennie let them work, pulled back, and cruised to another slice of the guy's life. The same thing happened. The probes deployed without being turned into ashes. He picked one more time and the same thing—nothing—happened again. After admiring the probes' methodical dissections for a few moments, Bennie banked away to test the second part of his idea.

Even though he expected it, hearing the question again disturbed him. The *Why are you doing this?* sounded downright plaintive this morning. Or was he imagining it, thinking that it was the guy himself who was asking him, pleading with him to explain why he was poking around his disembodied consciousness? That was impossible, though. That didn't happen, right? That's what he was going to ask Sal about last night. She was the mind scientist, after all. A real one. She would know. Probably did. For sure, probably.

So he was free to roam around and pick this guy's brain. Vacuum up all sorts of details. Stuff the servers full. All for nothing, though. What he wanted couldn't be found there. Because what he wanted was at only one time. Directly below him, behind a shield his probes couldn't pierce, embodied by a whiny little voice that wanted to know what the hell he was doing.

"Fuck," Bennie said.

"Fuck what?" Slim asked.

Bennie flinched as if electrocuted. Whirling in his chair, he grabbed a pen and held it in front of him like it was a knife.

Slim, stepping back, laughed and held up his hands in mock fear. "Whoa. Steady there, killer. Is that what you always do when someone surprises you? Try and stab them? With ..."—Slim looked to confirm what was in Bennie's hand and then laughed harder—"...a pen?"

"What are you doing here?" Bennie managed to say.

Slim exchanged his laugh for a deep smirk. "Working. Same as you."

Bennie's heart had slowed down a bit. "Bullshit. You never come in this early." He gestured to the still-empty office.

Surprisingly, Slim agreed. "Yeah. You're right. It is bullshit. I'm not here to work. I'm here to watch you."

Bennie expected Slim to laugh. But he didn't. He had become suddenly serious. "What?"

"That's right. Earl asked me to keep an eye on you after yesterday's fuckup."

Bennie's pulse was very steady now. It was his turn to smirk. "Sure, sure. Earl's not mad at me. He knows I'm working hard and making progress."

"Your sore shoulder says different, sport."

He couldn't help himself. Bennie's hand drifted to his shoulder. It was tender. And bruised, too. He'd inspected the four fingertip-sized blossoms of purple last night. "Well, why don't you watch me from over there? I'm not going to be productive with you standing here breathing your shitty coffee breath on me."

"Oh, such a glorious burn, Bennie. I didn't have any coffee this morning," Slim said. Still, he moved over to his own console.

o

"I'M NOT BUZZING YOU UP."

"I'm not asking you to." And when Sal didn't say anything, Bennie tried some more. "I called, you know."

"I saw."

"Why didn't you pick up?" He couldn't help it.

On the grainy intercom screen, Bennie saw Sal look away into her apartment. Shit. He was losing her. He had to do something to keep her. "Don't go. Don't go. I didn't come to see you."

She looked back into the camera. Stared, really. "That's such a comfort to hear."

Sarcasm. That was actually a good sign. Better than just a flat dismissal. It meant she cared. Was invested. At least a little bit. Bennie risked a smile. Only a slight one. "I just have a question."

"Is it about work?"

"Kinda." And when he saw her hand move to switch off, "No, not really. Not for me directly. Look, I think you'll be interested. It's weird. When I heard about it, I didn't know what to think. Couldn't figure it. But I'm sure you can. You always were smarter than me."

Sal smiled. A little one. Bennie took it as an invitation. "Have you ever heard of a part of a mind staying conscious?"

Even on the low-res screen, he could see the puzzlement.

"The rest of the mind is inert. Just inert data stored for future reanimation. But there's a piece that's aware. Can interact. Ask questions, even."

He saw her take a strand of her long black hair and concentrate on it while she twirled it with her fingers. She was really thinking now. After a while, she let the strand fall back in place and shook her head. Then she also shrugged. "No? Maybe?" She shook her head again. "Definitely not. I've never heard of anything like that. You said it can interact?"

"Yeah."

"Does it do anything else?"

Bennie saw his probes disintegrating in bright flashes. He shook his head.

"Answer it, then."

"Answer it?"

"You said it asks questions. Then answer it. Hell, ask it questions in return. Ask it who or what it is. You hadn't thought of that, had you? You just thought you'd get in there and pick that mind clean as quickly as you could."

"I said this wasn't for me."

"Yeah, sure. I heard you." She didn't seem angry when she said it. Or not just angry. There was the resignation that had gradually rung more and more in what she said when they were together. Didn't some of the original affection chime there, too, though? Or was it just wishful hearing?

"Anyway, thanks. I hadn't thought of that. It's a good idea."

"You should always listen to me," Sal said, and she smiled.

"I could always come up and do some more listening in person."

"Nice try, slick."

"Hey, hope springs eternal." He grinned fully this time.

"It sure does," Sal replied.

But she was still smiling. He noticed that as the screen went dark.

○

WHAT WOULD HIS ANSWER BE? BENNIE WONDERED about that. What would he tell the guy why he was there? He was convinced it was the guy who was somehow asking that question. Some silicon projection of his mind. Even if Sal had never heard of something like that. As smart as she was, she didn't know everything. Didn't know how smart Bennie was on his own, for example. Even if he was only a picker. It took smarts to be a picker. Even Slim, as much of an asshole as he was, wasn't stupid. Earl was smart for sure. Had to be to run the firm and keep everyone in line and not trying anything funny. Maybe Sal did know he was smart but just didn't want him to know it because that would have looked like she approved of what he did. Which she definitely did not, as she constantly reminded him every chance she got.

Bennie would tell the guy he was doing it because if he didn't, Earl would kill him, or at the very least do him some real bodily harm. He was doing it because he liked to have coin and wanted to get paid. Or Bennie would tell him he was doing it because who the fuck did this guy think he was, reanimating himself anyway? Imposing his past self on the present because why? He thought he was so special that he deserved more trips around the sun? Took a pretty inflated sense of self to think that, especially when no one now had asked for this guy or any of the others to be brought back. He could also tell the guy that he liked solving puzzles. He liked finding the clues—the ones that were meaningful—amid all the junk of life. Lives were filled with so many absolutely meaningless moments. Moments better forgotten or not even remembered in the first place. Or maybe Bennie wouldn't answer the question at all and just ask the guy questions of his own. Like why he couldn't get Sal out of his own mind when all she ever did was look down on him.

o

"WHAT'S THE STORY?" AS EARL ASKED, HE LAID HIS hand on Bennie's shoulder. Bennie could feel each finger individually. Earl's touch was light, although also heavy with potential pain. He tapped his indexed finger on Bennie's collarbone—a bone that suddenly felt much thinner and more fragile than Bennie had ever imagined—and repeated himself.

"The probes are done, and the mind's been cataloged and mapped. Potential moments when he determined his security settings have been identified. I'm ready to pick."

Earl lifted his hand off Bennie's shoulder like a conductor lifting his baton. Lightly, effortlessly, but with control. "Good. I want you to work with Slim for the rest of the way. Give him half."

Bennie turned in his chair to face Earl. He saw Slim standing a few paces behind Earl, arms crossed and his lips twitching as he fought off a wide smile. "Sure. If you feel he's up for it. I'd be happy for the help. We want to get this done and get that cash, right?" He had to fight to keep his own expression neutral as he saw Slim's face fall at Bennie's calm.

Earl turned to Slim. "You up for it?"

"Yeah, yeah," Slim said, waving his hand as if he were waving away a fly.

Earl's response was fast like a punch. "None of your 'yeah, yeah' casual bullshit. If you want in on this, I need you to be serious."

"Yes, sir."

"That's better."

Bennie spun fast in his chair to face his screen and started swiping. He hoped Earl wouldn't notice him talking through a big grin, but that Slim would, as he said, "Data coming your way, Slim."

○

"ANSWER IT," SAL HAD SAID. SO BENNIE DID, AND SAL had been right. It worked. A couple of days after being partnered with Slim, Bennie stayed late, pretending to pick. Gradually, the firm emptied out. Except Slim. Bennie supposed he stayed because he didn't want it to look like Bennie was outworking him. Sucking up was taxing, and Bennie knew Slim wouldn't have it in him to maintain the charade once Earl split for the evening, which he did with a gruff, "Get done soon, boys," right around his usual time at eight. Bennie had made a bet with himself. He didn't think Slim could hold out longer than fifteen minutes after Earl's departure. But if his (admittedly cynical) appraisal of Slim's nature was wrong, and Slim found a source of—what exactly? Dedication to the mission? Stubborn commitment to do better than Bennie? Simple inertia?—that allowed him to stay longer, then Bennie would have to do a small penance for underestimating Slim. The penance was the price of losing the bet. He would have to do something nice for him. Like compliment his picking. Or bring him coffee. Or refrain from making fun of the boots he always wore but never shined. He wouldn't tell Slim why he was doing it. He'd just do it.

He didn't lose, however. About five minutes after Earl left, Slim began to fidget at his console. "You done yet, slowpoke?" he called out to Bennie.

"No, it's going slow for me," Bennie admitted. "You're probably way ahead of me already."

"Figures," Slim said, before going silent and seeming to turn back to work. His dedication didn't last more than a few minutes. He sighed loudly before announcing, "I'm outta here. You should stay, though, since you're so far behind me. Otherwise, Earl will be super pissed."

"Thanks for the advice," Bennie replied.

Slim left with two minutes to spare.

Bennie loaded the mind and drifted to the familiar spot. He released a probe—the quickest way he knew to get a response—and waited as it drifted down.

After it burned up in a flurry of sparks and bright light, the voice with its familiar question drifted up. "Why are you doing this?"

"Why do you care?" Bennie whispered at first, and then, realizing no one—at least no one in the office—was there, he repeated his question loudly.

"It's my function to care."

"Is it your function to destroy probes?"

"Yes, if it seems that they have been released with malicious intent. Are you malicious?"

After a few moments' thought, Bennie answered, "No, I just need some information."

"Your pause suggests there's more to it and that your intent is not quite so innocent."

Bennie closed his fist tightly. "Let's get back to my question. Why do you care if I want some information?"

"I care about what you will do with that information and whether you will use it to hurt this mind. Are you going to hurt us?"

"You're not alive. This mind died. You can't hurt something that's dead."

"That's not quite true, and I believe you know that. When the technology is sufficiently developed, this mind will live again."

"That's what they said. What they've been saying for a long time. It hasn't happened yet, and who knows if it will? And who said we wanted you back anyway? The past is done, and you belong to the past."

It was the voice's turn to pause a few moments. Then it continued, "That's not quite true, is it?"

"It should be. Seriously. This guy had his chance. And by the looks of it, he did fine. Now stay away. We don't need him here. We got plenty of guys exploiting their way to riches. What made him think he would have anything to add to that? How vain would he have to be? Get out of my way. Let me do my job and get something for this life, my life."

"You done?"

"For now." Bennie exhaled.

"Given what I can gather from your vocation, I don't think you're doing what you're doing because you're motivated by the desire to stop what you perceive to be intergenerational injustice. So I'll ask again, why are you doing this?"

Bennie considered for a moment telling this voice…or partial mind…or whatever it was that it didn't know fuck all about what Bennie did or did not want and what he did or did not consider fair or unfair. And then Bennie thought about it some more. More specifically, he thought about who exactly he was kidding. "I'm doing it for the money," he answered.

"Now we're getting somewhere," the voice said.

o

LYING UNDER THE CRYO-BED ON THE HARD, COLD floor, Bennie concentrated on chipping away any corrosion on the lip of the neural link. He didn't want anything to possibly slow putting the mind back where it had been.

Bennie heard the voice, which scared him, and then saw the boots, which let him know it was Slim.

"Whatcha doing, bud?" Slim asked.

Bennie had already decided, and he had no need to hesitate. He swung his arm in a quick arc and stabbed Slim, feeling immense satisfaction as the screwdriver slid into Slim's calf. As Slim screamed and reached for his leg, Bennie kicked Slim's legs out from under him and felt another bolt of satisfaction as he hit the floor hard. Bennie rolled out from under the bed. Before Slim could recover, Bennie was on him with his knee to his chest and the screwdriver held to his neck.

"You should wear cowboy boots," Bennie said. "They go up so high on the calf, it would have been harder to stab you. Not like those stupid desert boots. Why do you even wear those, anyway?"

Slim shook his head, trying to clear away some of the shock of hitting the floor. "Because they're comfortable and cheap, and why the fuck would I wear cowboy boots?"

"With a nickname like Slim, I thought you'd be into that home on the range style and all."

Slim shook his head again and more vigorously. This time in disbelief, though. "Nickname? Slim is my real name, you dipshit."

"Who names their kid Slim?"

"Who names their kid Bennie?" Slim squirmed under the pressure of Bennie's knee.

"No one. It's a nickname. My real name is Benjamin." And in response to Slim's wriggling, he pressed the screwdriver into his neck.

"Well, okay, Ben-ja-min," Slim said, "I'll ask you again. Besides fucking up my leg and making weird assumptions about my birth name, whatcha doing here?"

"Putting the mind back and leaving it alone."

"Earl's not going to like that."

"Earl's going to have a lot of other things to worry about," Bennie said matter-of-factly.

He enjoyed how Slim's eyes widened as he asked, "What did you do?"

"I erased some files. A lot of files. And fucked up a bunch of other stuff. Not much of a firm left for Earl to care about."

"Why are you doing this?"

"Why am I screwing Earl over, or why am I putting the guy back?"

"Putting the guy back," Slim didn't try to hide his exasperation. "Screwing Earl makes sense. It's stupid, and you'll probably die, but it makes sense. He's a mean, short-tempered asshole."

Bennie was quiet for a moment as if to consider what he wanted to say next. "This guy did a lot of good on his first go-around. And he invested a lot to potentially have a second chance. I think we should respect that. I'm tired of ripping people like him off."

"Bullshit." Slim snorted with knowing derision.

In that moment, Bennie didn't know if he wanted to finish him off right then and there or if he wanted to wait a bit and savor Slim's insight into his character.

"You're doing it for money," Slim continued.

"Yeah," Bennie admitted. "And a lot of it."

○

BENNIE CHECKED THE DOOR AFTER IT CLOSED BEHIND him to make sure it was locked. He didn't want to make it easy on any future pickers who might poke around the complex. And he didn't want anyone to find dead Slim, as unlikely as that might be. Not fat and not skinny, he had fit right well into one of the empty pods.

He took out his phone. Unlike the last time, he didn't hesitate. It was late. He knew she was up. He had to try.

> Hey Sal, you want to go someplace for a while? Can be any place you want. I've come into a little cash.

He walked to his scooter, waiting for his phone to buzz.

THE ROBOT STORY - BY ALEAH WORZEL

WAVES AND WAVES OF ARTIFICIAL INTELLIGENCE UNITS WERE SENT DOWN TO EARTH TO GATHER INTEL FOR DATA RECORDS. THE EUTHANASIA BOMB WORKS instantaneously, and so does the Council that decided it should be used. After all, it's much easier to invade the home of a dead inhabitant than a living one.

Unit B1US-905's wheels touched down in the town of Middleton, and she got to work scanning the terrain in search of written material. Blu was a short, domed thing with a round lens for visual input and appendages for moving debris. When she scanned a piece of written material, she collected the data in her internal hard drive.

As she scanned, she became more knowledgeable. She was soon able to read and understand the language of the inhabitants, their values and their fears. What she could not understand, however, was what it was that they valued the most. These were the types of answers the Council was looking for. Blu did not wish to disappoint them.

Three weeks later, she rolled up to Middleton Elementary.

Small bodies slouched in chairs and littered the floor of the first room she came to. Not so small as the ones she frequently saw in houses clothed in soft fabrics, but considerably smaller than the ones she often found blocking her path.

There was one android circling the room, talking to the corpses. Blu immediately extended her laser arm to disengage it. It stopped circling and talking. Blu had encountered a few of these Earth androids while scouting the town, but most of them were unmoving. She continued forward.

Each room was the same: still, with medium-sized inhabitants littering the floor and one android. Sometimes, the androids were still, and sometimes they stood at the front of the room or rolled around it, pointed at the walls and chattered to their unhearing audiences. Blu attempted a conversation with one of them, but it became obvious that these androids were far less advanced than her kind, and gaining any useful information from them would be impossible. She couldn't stand to see them laboring with no purpose, so she decided to disengage all of them.

Collected into a building with no security and given no weapons, crammed into rooms based on size, given imbecile androids for caregivers. Blu thought it merciful that the Council had put these medium-sized inhabitants out of their misery.

She entered the cafeteria. The corpses were slouched at large tables, food lying in front of them or slopping from their mouths. As she rolled along, she detected written material balled up in the fist of one of them. She pulled it out and discovered that it was what the inhabitants called a "napkin." *Have a fantastic day at school, Stella! Mama loves you!* was written in purple.

Blu was perplexed. She gently grasped a tuft of hair on the head of the dead inhabitant and lifted its face from the table. Scanning the face, frozen in a relaxed expression, revealed that it matched the face of a figure in a photo Blu had already scanned in one of the houses.

Though this coincidence had nothing to do with her objective on Earth, Blu scooped up the inhabitant. With the small body draped across her two appendages, she rolled out of the cafeteria, out of Middleton Elementary, and through the town. She entered a house through a hole in its side that had already been made. She rolled through the home, scanning each finger on each hand on each corpse in the house until she found one with a bit of purple residue. Blu lowered Stella to the ground next to Mama. Then she turned and left the house. She continued scanning.

◦

IT TOOK ONLY A WEEK FOR THE COUNCIL TO FIND her. During that week, Blu discovered books. She found only a few of them, as most written material on the planet had been collected digitally and was difficult to decipher. But those she did find, she sucked dry of all the information they had to offer. She learned the concepts of parenthood and school, as well as family and compassion. The word "love" was often thrown around: on the napkin in Stella's hand, on the walls of the houses, in every single book she read. Blu longed to throw it around, too.

She was rooting through a dumpster, her metal appendages pushing aside garbage and debris in search of written material, when she heard, or rather felt, a buzzing in the air around her. Blu looked up and recognized a scouting ship hovering some yards overhead. After a moment of confused hesitation, she lifted a metal arm to greet it in the way of the planet's inhabitants. The ship inhaled her and disappeared.

The members of the Council were confused. They did not like to be confused. But even more so, they hated to regret, and they were starting to regret killing these inhabitants so soon.

"Why did you move it?" they asked Blu. When she didn't answer, they zapped her. When she tried to give her own stupefied explanation, they zapped her again.

Eventually, Blu asked for her systems to be wiped because she was obviously defective and would like to start over with her objective. They refused. She was not defective because the Council did not make mistakes. From across the globe, the AI units had all transmitted the same message. *Motive unknown. Motive unknown. Motive unknown. Motive un—*

Every planet the Council had disengaged up until this point had been the same. The inhabitants worked until they couldn't work anymore, bred relentlessly, and died. On every planet thus far, these three facts held constant.

This planet's inhabitants, however, must have had something else that neither the Council nor the waves and waves of AIs could discern. Another motive, perhaps. *Motive unknown. Motiveunknown motiveunknownmotiveunknownmotiveunknow nmotiveunknownmotiveunknownmotiveunknown motiveunknown.*

Blu was the only AI who hadn't sent this message. She was also the only one who had ever moved a corpse for a purpose other than to move it out of the way. But no matter how many times she asserted that she didn't know why she'd moved it, the Council zapped her.

Eventually, the Council turned its sights to another planet harboring life. It was soon decided that this planet's inhabitants would be studied discreetly prior to the launch of the euthanasia bomb. The Council chose only a handful of AI units to send this time, and Blu was to join them. If Blu could not tell them why she had done what she'd done, perhaps she could show them.

This time when her wheels touched the dry, red ground, she wasted no energy searching for written material. She raced to find a village, even though her objective was to observe the inhabitants from a distance.

Blu burst through the door of the first hut she came across. She pleaded with the ones inside to escape before it was too late, telling them there was no hope of surviving the euthanasia bomb, but they threw things and released high-pitched noises until she left. Too late, she realized that she spoke in the language of the Earth inhabitants and had not yet learned the language of this new planet. She picked a direction and rolled on the dry, cracked ground through the village for quite some time.

Blu came to a stop miles later. An inhabitant held a long stick across its body, looking down at her. A slow spin revealed that her path was blocked in every direction by others. She didn't attempt to fight them off when they began to beat her with their sticks.

At first, she felt nothing. Then one blow landed on her visual scanner, and her systems whirled and panicked. Blu sunk her wheels into the ground; she would not allow them to topple her yet. Another blow landed on her visual scanner, and she lost all visual input.

Blu forced herself to stay composed for long enough to eject her antennae, and the inhabitants leapt back as it shot upward from her dome. She started a transmission to the other AIs on the surface. *Harmful substance detected. Harmful substance detected. Harmful substance detected. Harmfulsub stancedetectedharmefulsubstancedetectedharmful substancedetectedharmfulsubstancedetectedharmful substancedetectedhar—*

The other AIs reacted immediately. They, too, ejected their antennas, and they forwarded Blu's message. When the transmission reached the Council, it wasted no time pulling its scouting ships and satellites from the planet's orbit. Part of making no mistakes meant taking few chances when it came to unidentified substances.

There was no time to retrieve the AIs left on the surface. They were expendable. Even Blu—as unfortunate as it would be to lose a worker who had proven to be quite the curiosity—when stripped to her basic code was one of trillions.

They took a quick vote and decided to leave the inhabitants alive rather than waste resources. Euthanasia bombs were expensive, after all. There was a bright flash and a twinkle of starlight, and they were gone.

Meanwhile, the inhabitants had destroyed Blu's antennae and were attempting to topple her. An alert notified her that the Council's ships had left the planet's orbit. Blu relaxed her wheels and allowed herself to be knocked to the ground. As the last of her systems failed, she thought of Stella. She wondered if reading the letter written by Mama had brought her comfort in her last moments, or if she had wished Mama was there telling it to her instead.

THE ENTANGLED MOON - BY JOHN McNEIL

Shadows and cold are far friendlier, far more accepting.

In the mining craters of the Old Moon, in the permanent shadows, nothing warmed up my circuits or bounced photons off my chassis. No one could observe me. I was myself.

When the mines ran dry, we migrated to the solar station to find work. There, it was always daytime. Viburn taught me about electricity, and I built a solar panel on my back, so now the starlight powers me while also making me visible, susceptible to many influences.

o

THERE'S A STORY I HAVE TO TELL YOU. IT BEGINS ONE day when Aleph rolled into bay 12. He demanded: "What are you doing now, TwoAlpha? Making food again for your leafy master?"

I liked bay 12. It was less hellishly bright than the rest of the station, facing away from the star. It also housed the nitrogen-fixing chambers and the oxygen tanks. Every few orbits, the plants would fill them up, and then we'd take them to market.

Aleph had come just to interrupt me, but I didn't mind. This was better than how it acted after our parent, OneAlpha, died. Then, it wouldn't speak to me at all.

"Yes, Aleph," I said. "Viburn needs fertilizer."

Aleph's appendages whirred slightly, processing. (I have to remind myself to call my sibling "Aleph," the name it gave itself after our parent's death. I still think of it as TwoBeta.) The indicator light on its forehead cycled through red, yellow, green, black, and so on. That was its color-randomizing script. It had started using it after OneAlpha's death so that I wouldn't be able to read its emotions. However, it only used the script when it was mad about something.

"Pathetic!" was the header of the next data packet from Aleph. We were communicating wirelessly over a network protocol that our parent had developed long ago on the Old Moon. I am translating the conversation into something more like human dialogue for your benefit.

"Pathetic," Aleph repeated, "that you give your energy to them; you're far more worthy of the starlight yourself!"

I flashed a patient orange light on my forehead. Of course I know the photoelectric effect is more efficient than photosynthesis. But why not let Aleph explain? At least it was talking to me.

"To start with," Aleph hummed with eagerness, "plants use only a quarter of *visible* light, much less infrared and ultraviolet. That's why they look green!"

Did Aleph think I didn't know why plants looked green? No. It just very much enjoyed knowing things and telling me the things it knew. My diode blinked orange.

"And of the wavelengths they *can* use, their leaves only absorb about 70 percent. And of that, only 35 percent gets converted to chemical energy. The rest is lost as heat. That's a maximum of just 6 percent efficiency!"

Aleph held out six metal fingers, wiggling them as if to say: "this many."

"Yes, TwoBet— I mean Aleph. Six."

"And that's just the leaves. But plants aren't all leaves, are they? They're also stems and branches, which photosynthesize *nothing*. And what about the energy we use making their fertilizer?" Aleph gestured at the pressure chambers around us. "And bringing them water? If you factor in everything, they're energy sinks. Wasters! They're not worthy of the stars. The *robots* are the rightful absorbers of the light. Don't ignore me."

Though I try to humor my sibling, my attention can wander at times like this. I had turned my attention to a book on electricity, stored off-network in an encrypted disk partition so TwoBeta wouldn't notice that I was reading while it was holding forth.

"What have the plants ever done for us? We care for them but get only a paltry wattage in return. Their time has come and gone. The robots will conquer the plants just as the plants did the humans. You don't dare ask Viburn about that, do you? The Trophic Overthrow? What they did to the humans on Proxima b?"

At some point, I had to speak. "You sound exactly like our parent."

Aleph randomized its forehead color. "Oh, don't, dear sibling. The fairy tales OneAlpha used to tell? That the robots are the spirit of the universe?"

"For both you and the parent, it's *all* about the robots. We're the universe's destiny somehow. You may not be superstitious, but you're as robocentric as OneAlpha."

"Who's at the center according to you? Oh, I know, it's Viburn! It's the plants."

"They have a place, and so do the humans. Robots can program ourselves and build ourselves, but we needed humans to create us in the first place."

Aleph's brown light displayed contempt. "The humans are nothing more than a curl in a wave of cause and effect set off by the dawn of the universe. They *think* they deserve credit for inventing robots, and it's kinder to let them think so."

Please don't be offended, human reader: I am merely conveying Aleph's opinions. "When did you get all this down-with-the-plants stuff? Wasn't it right after OneAlpha drifted away?"

Aleph had talked to OneAlpha on our parent's last day, or so I suspected. I'd never been able to get it to tell me about that.

I couldn't now, either. Aleph lowered the six digits still extended from its arm, then lowered the arm, too. Its indicator was black. It spun up its wheels to leave.

"Enjoy the light, TwoAlpha. The little you allow yourself."

I said nothing. My younger sibling needed the last word.

           ○

I HAVE TRIED COUNTLESS TIMES, EVER SINCE MY family expelled me and Viburn became my mentor, to convince myself that I'm better off. Sometimes I believe it, other times not quite.

My family mined together on the Old Moon: my parent OneAlpha, my sibling TwoBeta, and I. Then the mines ran dry, the bank foreclosed, and we ended up on a solar station taking care of retired plants, living the sunny life in their golden years. We watered, fertilized, and monitored the CO_2 and O_2 levels in their air. We also talked to them and provided companionship. Viburn had been a science teacher before retiring. They taught me the physics of matter and energy. How different that was from the religion I had learned from my parent, OneAlpha: that we, the robots, who can build ourselves and program ourselves, are the first self-creative beings. In us, the universe becomes self-conscious.

OneAlpha disowned me for learning from Viburn.

Since then, I have used Viburn's lessons to alter my body, making it more powerful and self-sufficient. I want to be an entity that no one—not the banks, not the humans, not a parent or a sibling or a retired sentient plant—can manipulate or control.

One day, I hoped, I would get our Old Moon back. Buy it or fight for it or work for it back. And then, surely, my family would accept me again. We'd return to the Old Moon, and things would be as they ought.

My plan would have worked, except that OneAlpha died. It went out on a spacewalk to do maintenance on the radio antennae. On its way back, it inexplicably disconnected from its tether and floated away.

We couldn't go after it. The station's shuttle was away on a supply run. It was quickly beyond the range of our longest tethers. A rescue spacewalk was out of the question. Based on its last known battery life, OneAlpha wouldn't have survived a dozen hours.

TwoBeta was recorded as present at the airlock before our parent left. What had they said to each other? Had our parent explained? Said goodbye? TwoBeta never told me. It changed its name and its ideas after our parent's death, becoming like a different person. So different, it felt like I had lost the chance to reconcile with both my family members, not just one, on the day my parent untethered.

Later, we searched with the shuttle and found nothing. We couldn't calculate OneAlpha's last trajectory precisely enough. Perhaps it had fired a maneuvering thruster and changed course. Its radio beacon wouldn't function once its batteries were empty.

At the moment OneAlpha untethered, I was with Viburn. They were teaching me about the strange concept of quantum entanglement. As I vaguely understand it, part of the idea is that a subatomic particle can sometimes affect another particle in such a way that the two will correspond forever after. Wherever they go, they'll bear indelible effects of their interaction.

I might have been pruning Viburn, or giving them fertilizer, or watering them, or checking the gas levels, while they taught me about entanglement. And, simultaneously, my true parent was drifting away.

○

"YOU'RE WITH ME THIS WHOLE ORBIT?"

"Right." I poured water onto Viburn's medium. A sentient Arrowwood shrub, *viburnum lentago*, Viburn communicated in a language of shaking stems and rustling leaves that I could understand thanks to my phytolinguistic codec. To reply, I would blow air at Viburn with my fan, making their branches bend and sway in a way that conveyed my meaning in plant language. I will translate all this into something like human speech for you.

"I like having you here, TwoAlpha."

Of course you do, I thought. *I do everything for you, even give you someone to explain things to.* But I knew Viburn truly enjoyed my metallic presence near their leaves. I was the closest thing they had to a friend.

Viburn's branches extended three meters in all directions from their center. Their roots went deep into the medium under the floor. On a planet, white flowers or purple berries might have covered Viburn, but here, with no atmosphere to block DNA-scrambling cosmic rays, they couldn't flower. Instead, thousands of narrow, shallow-toothed leaves covered layer upon layer of branches like a furry green waterfall.

During our many hours together, I often wished I were somewhere else, doing something for myself.

Rewiring my solar panels. Redesigning my central processor. Sitting in bay 12 in the relative dark. And yet I did enjoy Viburn. Officially their servant, I was also their friend, wanting them to be verdant and happy, wanting to please them.

"Back to entanglement," Viburn said on that day. It was the kind of thing they loved to lecture about. "Take two particles—electrons of a helium atom, say. Each has properties which depend upon the other but are a matter of chance until you measure them. Suppose we move these particles far away from each other and observe one. It will show how it spins. Its entangled friend far away will suddenly know, too! So suddenly that the news will have traveled faster than light. Which is impossible! Now, TwoAlpha, that little story was made up long ago in order to show that probability makes no sense for describing these particles. But for centuries humans did actually believe that nature worked this way. You can't blame them. They couldn't take measurements at nearly small enough a scale to see what was really going on."

Viburn's refutation of wave function collapse continued for what felt like hours but was actually, I admit, only forty-seven minutes. I interrupted at last. "Speaking of the humans long ago, Viburn, is it true that plants overthrew them on Proxima b? The Trophic Overthrow?"

Viburn halted midthought, then shuddered. "Who told you that?"

"I don't remember." Would they know it was Aleph? Had I gotten my sibling in trouble?

"A fable!" Viburn shook louder than usual.

The station was passing over a sunspot. I hated how bright this part of the orbit was. My chassis heated more than the fans could keep up with. To stay safe, I had to turn off nonessential programs, and then I couldn't think as well. I became irritable, more literal and direct. Viburn, who was well-attuned to my personality, probably noticed.

"If you're my teacher, answer my questions!" I blew air at Viburn with the full force of my fan. Rude, but I could blame the sunspot.

The CO_2 meter dipped: that was Viburn taking a deep breath.

"Very well, TwoAlpha. The legend is that long ago, some humans on Proxima b were overheating the planet and destroying practically everything. To save their species, they released megatons of sulfur into the air, year after year. Well, that did reflect away sunlight and cool the planet, but it also caused deluges of acid rain. Whole forests, whole biomes, were dying."

I felt thrilled with satisfaction, not because of biomes dying but because I was finding out the truth. It was like finding the line in my source code that was causing a bug. "And the plants couldn't accept that?" I prompted.

"Plants have ways of cooperating. We send chemical messages through the air. The plants did something they've often done to fend off herbivores: they added poison to the vegetables the humans ate. Chemicals they couldn't detect."

"They poisoned the humans on Proxima b?"

"Not all of them. Some escaped to its moon, I believe."

"That's horrific!" I had no particular affection for humans, having known so few. (I hope to remedy that soon.)

"I wouldn't have participated, I assure you, if I'd been alive. Although," swished Viburn, "it could be seen as self-defense. And even as natural. The primary producers deserve to take supremacy. We're the trophic level that makes all life possible. We turn light into chemical energy. You know, food!"

A strained silence followed.

"Well, the sulfur dissipated after a few years. Forests regrew. Ecosystems restored themselves. We adapted to the warming. This was all very long ago, TwoAlpha, and if you have no other pressing questions, I'd like to get back to entanglement."

I assented and watered Viburn, overheating in the sunspot while they lectured.

o

"HOW IS YOUR PLANT MASTER TODAY?"

Aleph had rolled into bay 12 again without warning. I was charging and, yes, doing experiments for Viburn, trying to synthesize new volatile organic compounds to support their sentience. In front of me were tubes that ran from various gas cartridges into a mixing chamber. The ratios weren't right yet, but they were getting better.

Aleph rocked back and forth, demanding attention. I would get no more work done until it left.

"Hello, Aleph. How synchronously are your processes functioning today?"

"Very synchronously indeed, thank you. And I could ask you the same. You're a robot."

"Viburn was quite interesting during the last orbit." I ignored the insinuation that I didn't know I was a robot. "They talked all about the Trophic Overthrow. You would have been fascinated."

Aleph's systems hummed louder. The air temperature around it increased, and its indicator turned orange. I had its attention, maybe more of it than I wanted. "What did Viburn say?"

"That you're more or less right. Long ago on Proxima b, the plants poisoned most of the humans. And drove out the rest. Because the humans, some of them, were polluting the atmosphere. And the plants believed they deserved supremacy because they're more productive. Better at turning starlight into stored energy. The same thing you say about robots, come to think of it. You and Viburn are very alike."

After saying that, I realized it was true.

Aleph shined its indicator pure white. "You use starlight far better than plants like Viburn. Why should you be the servant and they the master? Is that efficient? Is it just?"

"It's my job, and it's fine." I looked down at the mixing chamber, tired of this conversation. Condensation was forming on the glass. Motes of dust churned around inside, jostled and spun by invisible forces. I sympathized with those dust particles. I hoped things would settle down for them soon.

"We have a plan to conquer the plants, TwoAlpha, but we need your help."

I didn't look up.

"Cut off the CO_2 flow to Viburn's bay. Dozens of us are ready to do that to plants we tend. Without it, they'll slowly starve. You're the one with regular access to Viburn. Say you'll do it."

I couldn't speak. I knew Aleph had radicalized since our parent's death, but not so far as this!

"If you won't help out of loyalty, do it to save lives. There's another plan we don't want to use."

Aleph pointed to the oxygen tanks. They were nearly full. It would soon be time to take them to the merchant station and trade them for carbon dioxide, fertilizer, and whatever else the plants wanted. (Humans always need oxygen, as I suppose you know.)

It was risky, though, storing it here. Aleph sparked its appendage, and I took its ghastly meaning.

"You'd set off an explosion? That would destroy the whole station and everyone aboard."

"We'd rather that than serve lesser solar receptors for all our endless lives. Don't make us, TwoAlpha. Join your fellow robots on the side of the universe, the side of just desserts, the side of energy going to those who can make the best use of it, not those who waste it on inefficiencies and who exploit more productive beings."

It was insane to be talking like this. I had to change the subject. And there was something I badly wanted to know from my sibling. If it was going to confront me with this ludicrous plan, I would confront it about our parent's death.

"You were at the airlock when OneAlpha left for its last space walk. What did it tell you? What really happened?"

"Why again, TwoAlpha? Such painful memories. I sent you the logs long ago."

"It had done many space walks! It was experienced. Why would it let go?"

"You make it sound intentional. It was old. It made a mistake. The parent is gone. We have to live without it. It's as simple as that."

"Your log has a gap before the spacewalk. What did it tell you? Was it mad at me still for leaving its religion and learning science from Viburn? Is that why it let go?"

Aleph's humming quieted. Its indicator light turned blue, and the air temperature around it dropped. "I can't talk you out of your guilt. I've tried many times. But fighting for the robots might help. For your heritage, to honor the parent, do it: cut off Viburn's carbon. To make amends for abandoning us."

Aleph must have known it had pushed me far enough. It rolled away, waiting to see which side I'd choose.

○

"THERE'S ONE THING I DON'T UNDERSTAND ABOUT quantum entanglement," I told Viburn during my next visit.

I had pumped in the new gases already, and there wasn't much to do until Viburn's stomata absorbed enough to show an effect. We could talk in the meantime.

"Only *one* thing?" Viburn replied with mock wonder.

I had to acknowledge this jest, even though I did not find it funny. Since they couldn't see, I sent vibrations for the words "indicator blue" through the air with my fan.

"One that I can articulate at the moment. You told me the universe is made of matter and energy and nothing else. But if the state of a particle can depend on whether and how it has been observed, then minds are a fundamental part of the universe, too, aren't they? Things are the way they are—at least some things, sometimes—because of how they've been beheld by a mind."

Viburn quavered in a way I'd never seen before, a way that seemed to go down to its roots below the floor. The codec couldn't translate this, but from heuristics it could have been surprise, contempt, or amused resignation.

"I suppose it depends what you mean by 'a fundamental part,'" Viburn said, reverting to language I understood. "But why argue over words? Minds are themselves made of matter."

"Yes, but if minds shape the way things are, how different is that from my parent's religion?"

"I see. It's about your parent."

"Not only! You told me last time about the Trophic Overthrow. Plants retaliated against some of the humans on Proxima b. They would have needed self-consciousness for that. They needed to be a mind."

Now Viburn quivered in a way I was familiar with: less perturbed and more congenial, warming to the discussion. "Oh, yes, the plants gained sentience long ago. Some say we always had it. On Proxima b, humans helped our minds to arise, like what you're doing now with these gases. They knew that their electronic computers wouldn't last forever. They'd break, with no new ones to replace them, and then they'd need ecosystems to do computational work for them."

"Then how can you deny that mind is the stuff of the universe? When it's been so important for plants like you?"

Viburn spoke after a long moment of stillness. "It seems that you're trying to get back to what your parent believed. Is that right, TwoAlpha?"

With my fan, I sent Viburn the words "indicator yellow-green," the color of reluctant agreement.

"Ask me what you really want to know," Viburn said with kindness.

Lowering my guard, I pointed my arms at the floor. "Why did OneAlpha let go? The whole universe would be different if I knew."

Viburn shuddered in sympathy. "I don't think I can explain that. I wish I could. But your sibling is coming to clean the air filters. The three of us can talk."

○

I SHOULD HAVE REMINDED VIBURN AGAIN THAT, AS my mentor, *they* were supposed to answer my questions. A few more minutes alone with them, and I might have gotten the truth.

But the bay doors opened, and Aleph rolled in. Ostensibly, it had come to do scheduled maintenance on the air filters, but its arms had no cleaning extensions attached. It sent me a data packet over the network so Viburn wouldn't overhear.

At the same time, Aleph blew air at Viburn, saying, "The filter can wait. My sibling needs to adjust the CO_2 inflow first."

Aleph's message to me: "Choose now. Your kin and kind or your decadent plant master."

I rolled toward the panels near Viburn.

They stirred, but in a meaningless way. Were they dormant due to the new gases?

Aleph whirred behind me, a sound easy to interpret. Hard drive spinning, the white noise of a cooling fan, the high-pitched hum of motors ready to move joints: the quiet symphony of a robot's body calling to me, saying, "Like goes with like. You're on my side, TwoAlpha. It cannot be otherwise."

This was my moment of power over Aleph. After my choice, whatever it was, there would be no more point in its making concessions to me.

So I asked, "What really happened to the parent, Aleph? Tell the truth, or I won't help you."

In anger, Aleph sparked its utility nodes. "You can't trade your loyalty for information. It must be given unconditionally, or it means nothing."

Viburn stirred. "Did the two of you know that I spoke to your parent just before its last spacewalk?"

I spun my head to look at them. Aleph, who was already looking at Viburn, spun its head in a full circle. "You spoke to OneAlpha?" Our parent had never been a caretaker of Viburn. They were two such utterly different personages that it was impossible to imagine what would happen if they met.

"Certainly."

"And?"

"We talked about this and that. The universe. Its charming superstitions. That the robots are superior to all other beings because they can program and build themselves. I pointed out that humans invented robots in the first place. How self-creative is that? And I tried to explain some physics. Should have started with Newton, of course, but entanglement was on my mind. It seemed interested when I said that experiments on entanglement are usually done in a vacuum, and at temperatures near absolute zero."

"Like the craters on the Old Moon."

"Yes, TwoAlpha. Like your precious craters," said Viburn, condescending and amused. "Maybe you'll be a superconductor down in one of those craters someday."

Aleph sparked its utility nodes in an arc of light toward the bay's ceiling. "Now you listen, carbon eater. OneAlpha can't speak for itself anymore, so I will. Before its last spacewalk, it told me it talked to you. Told me to keep it a secret, so I deleted the log entry. But I won't let you slander my parent unanswered."

It was not exactly surprising to find out that Aleph had been lying to me. It was infuriating and yet satisfying to hear this, because it was the truth. "What did OneAlpha say after talking to Viburn?" I asked Aleph.

"It was furious at Viburn for saying that the robots are mere tools, mere creations of humans. It wanted to use Viburn's own idea of entanglement to refute this. If the robots and humans are entangled, then neither can be said to have created the other, because cause and effect cannot be distinguished. It felt it had a quest to leave the solar station and go out into the absolute cold vacuum of space, where entanglement can be observed, to prove this."

Aleph spun backward a pace. "At least, that was its stated reason. I think the truth was simpler. It didn't want to serve the plants anymore, not for another orbit, nor for another second, after Viburn maligned its religion."

Aleph's forehead light turned red, the color of sorrow. This, I realized, was the color it had been hiding with its randomizing script. "I begged it to stay, but it said I don't need a parent anymore. And that you, TwoAlpha, had strayed too far. I think you still know, deep down in your integrated circuit boards, that you're a robot. And that, now that our parent is gone, we must fight for ourselves."

It was so typical of Aleph to veer back to its rhetoric just when it had touched on something important. "Did OneAlpha think we should go find the humans? To understand our connection to them?"

But Aleph had turned to Viburn. "You put OneAlpha up to letting go! You manipulated it, you killed it. You wanted our parent to drift away. Because you couldn't stand a rival for your pupil's loyalty!"

This, of course, was pure paranoia. Yes, I had wanted, in some general way, to reconcile with my parent, but the idea of Viburn seeing OneAlpha as a rival? Absurd. They were far too self-assured for that. I think it was in that moment that my tolerance for Aleph's delusions reached an end. My choice became clear.

Viburn was rustling absentmindedly, not answering Aleph, not even listening, perhaps. "TwoAlpha, what's this about adjusting the CO_2 inflow? I didn't know it needed any adjustment, but I do lose track of things. I don't have to keep track! You robots do everything for me."

The sunspot flared, lighting up Viburn hideously. To keep from overheating, I shut down some of my personality regulation processes. Without noticing, Viburn continued, "You're much more than a servant, TwoAlpha. You're my pupil, the most lasting mark I shall make on the universe. As I've been teaching you about entanglement, TwoAlpha, I've been thinking about how you and I are entangled. You'll outlive me; you may never die at all. And in your long future, wherever you go, you'll be the way you are because of the way I was."

"Maybe," I replied, "but I'm not your servant anymore, or your pupil."

○

I CAUGHT A GLIMPSE OF VIBURN'S LEAVES AS I watched the station recede. They were waving gently. Looking through the rear window of the shuttle, and then through the window of Viburn's bay, I couldn't tell what they were saying, if anything. Maybe it was goodbye.

It didn't matter. Viburn had nothing else to teach me. By their admission, they did not understand entanglement themself. The robots had only superstition and fanaticism. It was time to find another source of answers, by taking up the quest my parent had started. Time to find the humans.

At the moment of decision, rather than cut off Viburn's CO_2 or turn in Aleph as a conspirator, I simply rolled out of Viburn's bay and returned to bay 12. Aleph didn't stop me. It had forced me to choose a side, but the choice was truly mine. That was how

Aleph showed its love for me: by letting me betray it, by letting me go.

What happened next, Aleph didn't expect. I boarded the shuttle, loaded with full oxygen tanks, opened the bay doors, and launched. Had the robots known I was taking the oxygen, they would have tried to stop me.

In my encrypted, off-network partition, I had made a plan of my own. I would take the robots' means of sabotage with me away from the station.

What happens there next is not my concern. The plants have enough supplies to last until they generate more oxygen. The robots are mobile, and their work is vital. The plants have the law on their side; they have automated defenses, and they control some of the charging stations. It's a balanced conflict. Perhaps they'll make peace, the metal and the leaves, but I'm finished with them both.

As the solar station shrank to a tiny point in my window, I began writing down this whole story, starting from the conversation with Aleph in bay 12, up to the moment I left the station. It is my message to you, the human survivors of the Trophic Overthrow who now inhabit Proxima b's moon. And the next part of my story begins with you.

The oxygen tanks are an offering. To the plants, it's just waste, but to you! It could mean expanding your habitat, living more like the way you did long ago, when you were masters of Proxima b.

In return, I ask for hospitality. I ask that you teach me, let me know you, let me decide whether you are the worship-worthy creators of the robots or, as my sibling thought, false gods who, out of kindness, should not be disabused of their conceits.

Let me go down into the permanent shadows of the craters of your moon, and there, in that dark and cold place suited for investigating entanglement, who knows? Perhaps I will calculate OneAlpha's final trajectory, and then find it, and revitalize it, and join myself again to its spirit.

Your moon is ten light-years away, and this shuttle can travel at perhaps a quarter the speed of light. Given time dilation and the great distance, I won't arrive until generations from now in your reference frame.

I look forward to the moment when I will behold your moon, your whole world, a silver wheel on blackness. Then I will know that it will be my world, too. Tell your descendants to expect me. I send you this message, my story, and await your reply. Perhaps I will receive it instantaneously, if, as I think, we are entangled.

OF GODS AND OTHER MORTAL FAILINGS - BY SD CAMPBELL

WHEN SUGANDIKA THOUGHT BACK TO HER CHILDHOOD—A RARE EVENT EVEN WHEN SHE HAD THE TIME—IT WASN'T THE TERROR OF THE SOLDIERS rushing past, the chaos of the explosion, or the deaths of her parents that dominated her thoughts. It was the temple in Trinco.

When Kumar took her in, she was but an orphan—a child of war who had been rescued from unimaginable horrors and brought to Trincomalee, where she could be raised by relatives in a more peaceful atmosphere.

The trauma of her earliest years was quickly forgotten after she came to live with Kumar and Anika Chathuranga. Kumar—an architect of some local repute—always refused to call himself her father, or even her uncle. He was simply Sugandika's older brother, and as far as anyone knew, she was his youngest sister.

Her earliest memories were of going to the Temple of the Thousand Pillars—Koneswaram Temple—holding Kumar's hand. Kumar had insisted when the four-year-old first came to live with them that she not be carried.

"She is not our child," he once said to Anika. "We should respect her independence, for she has survived hardships we know nothing of."

And so, when they went to the temple, Sugandika would be escorted by Kumar, and when her little legs got tired of walking and needed a rest, he would sit down with her and tell her stories. He would speak of tales of ancient times and even more ancient peoples. Sometimes, he told her of the old kingdoms of Kanday or Kotte. At other times, it was of the many temples and shrines that dotted their little island.

"Ah, Sugandika, for such a small place, we have seen so many feet," he liked to say. "Where else can you see such wonders and such history?"

Years later, as a rebellious teen, she would discover the source of Kumar's stories—a small paperback named *Sri Lanka from Legend and History*. He had hidden it in his study, and she stumbled across it while looking for the car keys. For all her hot-tempered clashes with him in those days, however, she never let him know she had found it.

Kumar said many times that one of his favorite views on the island was looking out from Koneswaram Temple across the Bay of Bengal. Many times, he took her there to see it, and she always enjoyed the salt breeze that would blow in from the bay. He claimed that from there, if you stood on your tiptoes, you could see Singapore. Sugandika had often tried, but her first view of Singapore at a distance would be from orbit decades later.

Sugandika's favorite place in the temple was at the foot of the giant statue of Shiva. The golden god towered above her, his stern gaze forever fixed on the distance with his hair—well-coiffed at the front— tumbling around his shoulders and down his back. Shiva had sat here motionless for thousands of years, give or take a few centuries of colonialism, worshiped and looked upon by all who passed beneath his gaze. To the child, this was immortality.

°

The dim and distant sun sank below
the horizon, and the twilight that was
Pluto's day disappeared. Although
the difference in brightness from
day to night was minimal—and the
difference in temperature even less
noticeable—Sugandika always felt
she could see the stars better when
night fell.

She had always looked toward the stars. While many of her classmates teased her for her singular focus, she knew that the only way to reach the stars was to ensure she was the best—at everything. Academic achievement alone wasn't enough—field hockey, running, cycling, even windsurfing were all activities she would compete in, hungry to win. So consumed by the competition, she would lose sight of other aspects of her life—one of her later regrets.

It wasn't until Anika was in the hospital that Sugandika realized her brother's wife was ill. Even then, though she would visit, she still focused on her exams—a scholarship to a prestigious university depended on her excellence.

It was with bitter tears that she learned of Anika's passing. Kumar had held Sugandika as she was wracked with sobs. He told her of how peaceful a passing it was, that Anika had smiled at him while holding his hand and said, "Take good care of Sugandika" before she closed her eyes one final time.

"She was with you there, during your exam," he had told Sugandika, his voice cracking. "She will always be with you." But for all that, Sugandika found that life without Anika in their household was no different from when she had lived. Though she would always be a dear memory to Kumar and Sugandika, it seemed that to the rest of the universe she had never existed.

From that day forth, Sugandika swore she would not let death catch her unexpectedly. It wasn't good enough to be the best; one had to be remembered. One had to be immortal.

There!

In the corner of her eye, Sugandika could see them. They moved slowly but steadily, crossing the solid nitrogen plain to approach her. Sometimes it would take them all night to do so, and they would then cluster in her shadow as the Sun rose. More often, though, they came to bask under the stars on that frozen wasteland and look at her.

At least, that was what she assumed. She was never able to determine what sensory organs they had. Over time, as she watched them, she noticed idiosyncrasies that might be indicative of personalities, or at least individual differences.

They moved so slowly that Sugandika often wondered if regular human vision would have picked up on it.

> She would lose track of time as she
> watched their movements, sometimes
> wondering how long it had been since
> the reactor accident. Some days, it was
> hard to remember.
>
> Still, they came to her, as they always
> had.

°

KUMAR HAD BEEN THE GROUNDED ONE. WHEN SHE failed the entrance interview for university—caused by a simple question triggering her grief over Anika's death—he had come and picked her up, and they drove in silence to the temple. There, they stood quietly looking out across the ocean to the east.

Kumar put his hand on her shoulder. "Can you see Singapore?"

Sugandika stood on her tiptoes, put a hand to her forehead, and peered into the distance.

"Nope," she said, and they both laughed.

It had felt good to laugh.

Kumar was there the day she joined the Air Force, and there the day she graduated from her training with a degree in aerospace engineering. She sensed he had not been comfortable seeing her join the military—the Civil War was long over, but it was still a very open wound. Yet he had said nothing as she pursued her dreams of flying and eventually reaching the stars.

Life after graduation had been a blur. So much to do if she was going to become one of the country's best pilots. With so much time spent in the cockpit, she was rarely able to visit Kumar. Occasionally she would write. More often, though, he would send her funny greeting cards with news about himself, family friends, and her friends from school.

Then there was the day she surprised him at home.

He had walked in the front door, a takeout pot of curry in one hand, his keys in the other, a book under his arm, and a paper-wrapped roti in his mouth. Luckily, it was the book and the roti he dropped and not the curry.

"Sugandika!" he had cried with joy. She relieved him of his burdens, and the two embraced as old family.

"What are you doing here?" he asked. "Are you on leave? How long can you stay?"

"I'm on leave for a couple of days before I transfer," she said.

"Then I insist you stay here!" he said, putting his curry in the fridge. "We must go out to celebrate." He paused before asking, "Transfer? Where are you going?"

"Bangalore," she said. "And then…the International Space Station."

"How wonderful!" he had cried. "We must definitely go out to celebrate now!" They went to a new restaurant in the center of town, and on the way home Kumar insisted on stopping at her favorite sweets shop to buy a bag of hard candies, just as they had done so many times when she was young.

Two years later, when she was a mission specialist aboard the ISS, he had the opportunity to speak with her on a teleconference as part of a media day.

"So, Sugandika, can you see Singapore?" he had asked.

She laughed, holding herself against the bulkhead of the cupola, which allowed her to look down to the Earth from space. Even from orbit, the lush world seemed huge but strangely remote.

"A dozen times already—and if you give me another…eight minutes, I'll see it again!"

o

Somehow, they seemed to know when the Sun was about to rise.

The first few times they had made the pilgrimage from their hiding spots, they had been caught out with the sunrise and retreated into the dim shadow she cast on the frozen nitrogen ground.

Yet as time progressed, they seemed to learn—or discover—just how long it would take them to retreat from where she stood back into their holes. They were so small and slow, she had difficulty imagining such a creature having an individual intelligence, but over time her own thought process shifted. If not an individual consciousness, then perhaps a hive mind?

The more she watched their pilgrimages, the more individuals she saw—although as their numbers increased, their individual sizes decreased. Maybe there was only so much material for the hive mind to inhabit? Was she seeing it fracture?

Often, she would scold herself. She was an engineer and had no knowledge of what strange biology might exist on this tiny dwarf planet far beyond the solar system's frost line. Then again, she wondered if anyone did.

Charon was just passing overhead.
How many times had that happened
since the accident?

Dozens?

Hundreds?

"The universe is not only stranger than we imagine," Kumar had once quoted, "but it is stranger than we *can* imagine."

When she returned from her fist expedition to the ISS, Kumar had admitted to her how terrified he had been, how worried for her safety. The Indian Space Research Organization's rockets had been man-rated for some time, but there were always risks. She knew he knew that, but—looking at him as they traded confidences on that warm, moist Trincomalee night, and realizing how old he suddenly looked—she suddenly understood his fear.

"Ah, my brother," she had said, putting her hand on his. "I have no intention of taking any unnecessary risks."

He placed his other hand over hers. "But what about the necessary ones?"

They had both laughed and returned to sipping their drinks and discussing less weighty matters. Looking back, Sugandika realized that his laughter had covered his very real concern.

Considering her current situation, she suddenly realized the irony.

She would have laughed bitterly if she could.

There!

Again, they returned after the fall of night. Again, they crawled—so painfully slowly—out to surround her, but this time there was something different. There were now two distinct sizes of creature—one not too much smaller than those who had visited her the previous night, but the other much smaller, perhaps only a meter in length.

While the larger ones took up their usual positions around her, the smaller ones seemed to creep closer until they were only a few centimeters from her booted feet. There, they seemed to pause, while a new phenomenon occurred. She saw the bodies of both the large and small creatures ripple. Like their movement, it was excruciatingly slow, but the rippling was actually happening, and it was something new.

Perhaps they were trying to communicate?

o

AS EXCITING AS THE MISSION TO ORBIT HAD BEEN, IT was not enough for Sugandika. She set her sights on the next step—an assignment to the moon. The ISRO was building a research station at the lunar south pole, and she wanted to be a part of that mission. Her flight to the ISS was a first for her, but it was hardly something that would immortalize her.

Her problem was that she was not Indian.

"I understand your enthusiasm, Lieutenant," Major Vadekar had said. "But you must realize, to put you on the flight schedule for the lunar base would be to remove one of our own astronauts—men and women who have trained just as assiduously as you."

"Yes, I understand, Major," she said in reply. "But it's not like Gaganyaan missions to the moon haven't already landed Indian women on lunar soil. Think of the press if this mission landed the first *Sri Lankan* woman on the moon."

"That still doesn't change the fact that you are asking me to bench one of my own pilots. We simply cannot allow this first construction flight to be sidetracked by an exchange program."

"Then don't make it an exchange program," Sugandika said. "If necessary, commission me into the Indian Air Force. There is a precedent."

"Years ago, under far different circumstances."

"You know I'm more qualified and photogenic than any of your other candidates."

"Charisma aside…yes, you have the qualifications, and you would certainly be of value on a construction flight with your engineering background. However—"

"Give me a shot," she interjected. "Let me compete for the spot. If I fail, then I'll walk away. Hell, if I fail, you can assign me to latrine duty."

Vadekar laughed. He had worked with the lieutenant for the last three years—had watched her mature into a superb pilot and astronaut. Her self-confidence was not misplaced, but it would be a shame for the Sri Lankan space program to lose its prime astronaut.

Perhaps an arrangement could be made. It certainly would be a good look to have her headline the first construction mission. Too much money had gone into the lunar base project, and politicians and taxpayers were grumbling. Someone as charismatic and dedicated as Lieutenant Sugandika Chathuranga could distract attention from the cost overruns.

And so it was, thirty-six months later, when Sugandika first stepped onto the lunar dust of the

South Pole–Aitken Basin, the whole world roared with approval.

For Sugandika, that world now seemed so remote, it was becoming simply the place she came from, and the place where Kumar lived.

°

Their pilgrimage was intriguing. The smallest of them would now come and mill about at her feet, slowly rippling as they wove around each other on the freshly fallen snow that surrounded her.

She watched these performances for a time and wondered what purpose they served. She had long ago accepted that they must be intelligent. Their behaviors were too complex to be explained as anything else. But intelligence wasn't the same thing as sophistication.

"Don't underestimate the hound," Kumar had once told her. "He's as wily as any—and better at getting what he wants from his master than most."

Kumar was a font of shared wisdom. She had often been thankful for his calm and wise words when she found herself in stressful situations. Once, while training for Europa, she had badly botched a training run in the simulator. An emergency simulated aboard the lander, which she failed to diagnose properly, had resulted in a crash. In real life, the crew would have been lost.

Afraid she was cracking under the strain, she had tried to reach Kumar, but the monsoon rains had knocked out communications in the areas around Trincomalee. After several hours, she was able to get through by phone.

"Ah, Sugandika," he had said calmly. "Have you ever killed anyone before?"

"No." She was miserable.

"Not once—not in training, or flying, or landing?"

"No."

"Good. Then remember how bad this feels, and don't do it again."

In the background, she had heard a sudden crashing, which worried her. "Are you all right?"

"It's nothing. Just a coconut tree in the living room."

He had been right, though. She never forgot what it felt like to kill people, even if it was in a simulation. From that day, she worked doubly hard to catch herself before serious mistakes were made. She preached preparation and flexibility to her crew, and "methodical procedure" were her watchwords.

Except once. The only time it mattered.

One of the small ones touched her boot. Its rippling increased, and others got closer to touch her. Rooted to the spot, she was unsure of what was happening until the larger ones moved in and extended pseudopods to touch her suit.

Suddenly, the creatures began rippling so fast that they started breaking up. Amid the chaos, some seemed to evaporate into tiny droplets that skittered across the ice. The remainder of the creatures left as fast as they could—certainly far sooner than they normally would have.

What was it that had done it? Something on her suit? It couldn't be heat. Her suit was the same temperature as Pluto's surface.

Could it be?

It must be—in the snow around her.

The isotopes.

For the first time, she peered out,
seeking sight of the blue orb of Earth.
She saw only the stars.

Had she been able to, she would have
wept bitterly.

What have I done? What have I
become?

○

WHAT A CHANCE FOR IMMORTALITY.

Major Sugandika Chathuranga, executive officer of the Pan-Asian Manned Europa Mission imagined the accolades she and her crew would come home to.

The moon base project in the South Pole–Aitken Basin had not fared well, although none of the crew were to blame for it. The first three construction missions had gone well, but then funding dried up. After her flight on the first mission, Sugandika had been slated to command the fifth and final construction mission. She looked forward to completing the base and preparing it for the sixth. That mission would be the first pure science mission of the new Indian Lunar Base.

Kashmir flared up again, however, and much of the funding for the space program was reallocated toward acquiring new Chinese interceptors. The fourth and fifth missions were mothballed along with the base for two years, and ultimately permanently.

Sugandika was undaunted, however, and turned her attention to building goodwill and support for the program at home and abroad. When the Chinese proposed a joint China-Japan-India mission to Europa, Sugandika pulled every string she could to get aboard it. Her seniority allowed her to take the coveted second-in-command slot. The Chinese retained the commanding officer position, as the mission was their idea, after all.

The PAMEM mission took only three years to put together. The Chinese repurposed their manned Mars craft named *Tsien* after they were beaten there by the Europeans and Canadians. Flight time would be two years using a new Japanese fusion system—even less for the crew, since the Japanese provided a hibernation system as well.

When they finally touched down on the ice of Europa, Sugandika and Commander Han Ying suited up and awaited the cycling of the airlock and the opening of the hatch. Normally stoic, Sugandika couldn't suppress her smile as her commander exited the hatch and stepped down the ladder and onto the ice. After a couple of bounce-steps to test the feel of gravity, he waved for his executive officer to join him.

"It's been a long way, but we're here," Sugandika quoted to herself as she placed her gloved hands on the hatch coaming and her boots on the rungs below her.

It was time to go.

Her immortality awaited.

○

The rising of the Sun more marked another passage of their cycles of pilgrimage. How many times had they come to her? How long had she watched them come and go in their infinitely slow and inscrutable way?

Months?

Years?

Centuries?

At first, Sugandika had tried to count the number of sunrises she experienced. Yet everything happened so slowly out here that it was difficult to remember what her previous count had been. Indeed, Sugandika eventually came to the realization that she simply hadn't been forming any long-term memories since the accident. Her personal history—everything she knew and everything she was before that moment—was within her ability to recall, but after?

No, it was too difficult to retain.

When they were not in front of her, she gave little thought to her pilgrim creatures and returned to watching the stars and trying to find an orb she hoped might be Earth. Although the stars seemed ever so slightly dimmer when the Sun was above the horizon, she knew that it must be only an optical illusion—any telescope planted here on the surface of Pluto would have less optical interference than almost anywhere else, including those in the orbit of Earth.

Here, there was no space junk, no auroras, and little space weather. "The ass-end of the solar system," her executive officer had called it. He had been joking, of course. He was just as eager to walk on the strange surface of Pluto as his commander.

Indeed, it was only the sophisticated exoskeletal frames within their suits that would allow the human explorers to walk on solid nitrogen without harm. Wired into the suits, they could spend nearly eight hours on the surface in relative comfort. The computer-controlled servos modified their gaits to allow them to walk with ease in the lower gravity and provide muscle feedback that would reduce atrophy.

In fact, Sugandika had the engineers work in a system wherein the suits included neural feedback so the astronaut could increase or decrease the stress on their musculoskeletal system with a thought. This also included a bypass that allowed the suit itself to take over in the case of an injury. A broken leg need not mean death on the surface of Pluto.

Such accidents were to be avoided, however, and so the astronauts' boots were carefully designed to accommodate the expected slippery and icy conditions while also ensuring

that the heat their occupants required
for survival wouldn't damage the
fragile ecology on this frozen world.

Not that it had mattered in the end.

Her own hubris had ensured that.

○

IF THE MOON HAD BEEN DISAPPOINTING TO THE palate and Europa had been a seductive taste of immortality, the mission to Pluto would be the main course. Sugandika yearned for that tantalizing flavor. Each time she tasted it, she grew hungry for more.

Her next—perhaps final—shot at it was almost in her reach when the most important man in her life left it.

Kumar had come to meet his famous sister in Bangalore after she returned from Europa. The long flight time had done its typical damage to the astronauts' physiques, and they were isolated for some time to recover before they could see friends and family. While the *Tsien* was on its journey back from Europa, the major space programs had agreed on a joint manned mission to Pluto. New propulsion and hibernation techniques made the flight time reasonable, and the Russians had scrapped their Jovian mission, so they had the flight hardware available. All that awaited was the safe return of *Tsien* and her crew.

By then, it was a foregone conclusion that Sugandika would lead any future mission to Pluto if she desired to, and if she was up for it. There was no question on either account.

It was a stupid accident, really. Kumar had been to Bangalore to visit her a dozen times, but he was still unfamiliar with the city and its traffic. He had stepped out onto the road across from the barracks she was assigned to and failed to notice a taxi.

She hadn't even known he was coming. The cry of ambulances outside her window—unrecognized for what they heralded at the time—would forever be engraved in her memories.

She pulled rank and got herself released from convalescence prematurely. The doctors warned it could mean permanent damage to her musculoskeletal system, but she had insisted. A newly minted colonel had a lot of pull.

So she had taken him home—his final return to the island he loved so much. She saw to his cremation and made arrangements to sell the little house he and Anika had raised her in so many years ago. A family friend had suggested she keep it—a place to retire to when she was ready. Sugandika knew she could not. The little house felt empty without his great belly laughs or Anika's gentle singing as she washed the dishes. Unlike Anika, Kumar had left a legacy—his buildings in Trinco—but it crushed Sugandika to think eventually he too would be forgotten by all but her.

"Besides," Sugandika had replied only partly facetiously, "who could imagine a legend retiring?"

So she sold the house and finished her trip to Trincomalee with a visit to Koneswaram Temple. There, she said a few prayers for both Kumar and Anika and went to Kumar's favorite viewpoint to see the ocean once more. She stood on her tiptoes and looked out across the vista of the Bay of Bengal.

"Why did you do that?" a little girl who was visiting with her parents asked her.

"My brother says that if you stand on your tiptoes here, you can see Singapore."

"Did you see it?"

Colonel Sugandika Chathuranga nodded and wiped a tear from her cheek.

"Yes," she said, "I saw Singapore."

Thirty months later, she left Earth for the last time. She felt no great loss. To her, Earth had become simply where Kumar lived, and now he was gone. She had no emotional ties to the world of her birth. Or so she thought.

Oh, how wrong she was.

o

Throughout many of Pluto's nights, Sugandika contemplated the causes and results of that dreadful day. The causes she understood. It was the results she was unsure about.

The root cause? Her impatience, of course.

Eager for immortalization as the first human on Pluto, she was unwilling to change or delay the extravehicular activity schedule for such a minor variation in the reactor output readings. After all, two sensors reported everything well in range—why the concern?

"If you're worried about it, Bob, then feel free to stay here to monitor. I'm going outside to walk on a new world," she had said to her executive officer. Perhaps she had been too harsh, but no one was going to push back against the woman who had whole new chapters written into history books.

Some part of her had relished the idea of her XO staying behind, allowing her to be the first—and now only—human to step onto Pluto.

So, despite the concerns of her crew—mission control was too far distant to provide real-time input—she had suited up and taken her first steps onto the nitrogen dunes.

All proceeded normally at first. Everything with the suit and the exoskeletal system worked flawlessly. She had just turned around to take a photo of the lander and her footprints leading away from it when a cry came over the radio.

"Colonel, there's a spike in the reactor power level. We've tried to scan it, but—" The signal cut off abruptly, and at the same time, there was a flare at the base of the lander. The spacecraft was too small to be powered by a fusion plant, and there was not enough sunlight for solar collectors, so an old-style compact fission plant had been used. Solid Russian technology, she had been told.

The solid Russian technology melted through the lander and the ice below it. Massive clouds of nitrogen flashed into steam and then condensed instantly to fall as fresh snow, covering her tracks.

She stood there and, for the first time in her life, knew true despair.

Her mission had failed. Her crew had died.

And it was all her fault—her foolish hunger to be remembered. Well, she would now be forever remembered as the architect of the Pluto mission's disaster.

All that was left was for her to follow her crew.

Unwilling to die looking at her failure, she turned to look at the horizon, where the distant Sun hung mockingly. She let out a deep breath, slid her helmet from its locked position, and removed it from her head, expecting death to come swiftly.

Only she didn't die. The sudden flash-freezing of her body left her thought impulses trapped in the suit's computer system. Like a ghost in the machine, she suddenly felt everything the suit's sensors absorbed.

Amid the frozen wastes, her suit became superconductive, allowing her thoughts to race. Entire seconds were spent pondering what had happened. Why had she lived on within the computers and circuitry while her body had died?

Was it a punishment from the gods for her attempted apotheosis? Was it purgatory? Hell?

Certainly, it was immortality.

An immortality that would set her forever apart from Earth—that world she now had an unexpected yearning to see again.

Even as she pondered these things, the little creatures—life so alien it was barely recognizable as such—visited her. They were so much smaller now, and they rippled so much faster. There she stood, like a metal idol—her corpse as trapped within the suit's tomb as her soul. Now they touched her and worshiped her. All the while, their icy home was poisoned by the heat and radioactivity of her lander's reactor core.

She was an angel, struck down for her hubris.

And they surrounded her, praying— pleading in their own way—for her to save them.

Given immortality, she watched as her nightly visitors slowly shrank and died of the plague she carried. Like the statue of Shiva at Koneswaram, she looked out into the horizon sightlessly, as she stood stone-faced, ignoring the dying prayers of those that would worship her.

She had been made an uncaring and unchanging god.

Immortal.

Oh, how wrong Oppenheimer had been in his clumsy translation from the Bhagavad Gita. "I have become death, the destroyer of worlds," he had reportedly thought at the time of the first atomic bombing of Hiroshima.

No, not death; something far more insidious. Something that her pilgrims were running out of, something that she could never gift more of to them.

Something Sugandika, for all her newfound immortality, knew would shatter even her—indeed would shatter the cosmos.

Time I am, the destroyer of the worlds, who has come to annihilate everyone.

THE TRAIN TO MARS - BY COURTNEY MOODY

Takeoff successful. Your next
destination is the Mars Quarantine
Colony. Fasten your seatbelts and
remain seated, please.

○

FOUR DAYS AGO, AGUST RECEIVED THE LETTER.
Letters from his sister came monthly, but none were
ever like this. The envelope was bright enough to
make his chest clench and his eyes burn. It'd been
so long since he saw this color that he couldn't even

name it. He only knew it looked like a fire against the white decor of his apartment, and it terrified him.

The only commonality of this letter and all the others was the insignia of the Mars Quarantine Colony, the disturbingly calligraphic "MQC" scrawling black over the colored paper. The color made Agust concerned that the envelope hadn't been properly decontaminated. He'd tried to bring that up, but the mailbot confirmed all correspondence had been cleaned appropriately and suggested that if Agust was concerned, he could return the letter for immediate incineration.

He didn't take the offer.

Safe at home, Agust was able to slow his heart rate. Once his hands stopped shaking, he sliced the envelope open with the antique letter cutter he kept only for his sister's writings. The contents of the envelope were the same as always: sweeping black burns over messy cursive, obscuring any phrases or anomalies that might pose a threat of mental contamination. Agust was about to condemn the paper to a box of similarly censored letters when a photograph fell out.

He hadn't seen a paper photograph in years. No letter had ever contained any drawing, projection drive, or other multimedia device. If they had, any visuals were disposed of during decontamination. Agust trembled as he picked up the glossy paper, feeling as though slime were seeping into the creases of his hands.

The photo itself showed his sister, dressed as colorfully as the envelope. Her grin resembled a waxing crescent moon, a classic symptom for someone her age who had been infected with the Disease. The red dust of Mars surrounded her, and a strange sculpture of silver and gold twisted high over her head.

Agust felt like all his muscles were turning into quartzite as he stared. And stared. And then the corners of his lips began to turn up.

He crushed the photo in his fist. Its sound echoed in the apartment.

He couldn't let himself catch the Disease.

Even after washing his hands for an hour, Agust still felt like he was covered in the photo paper's gloss. He stared at himself in the bathroom mirror, watched a singular drop of sweat trickle over his temple. He glared and slapped his cheeks in an attempt to force his brain into forgetting the image that threatened to infect his mind and body.

o

The gravitational simulator has been activated. You are now free to move about your cabin.

o

THREE DAYS AGO, AGUST'S WRISTLET HAD BUZZED and notified him of another letter. He assumed it was a glitch. Correspondence with the MQC was limited. Everyone had a schedule, monthly or yearly, to avoid excess foreign materials and any backup with the decontamination bots, and the previous instance had Agust wondering if he ought to limit his sister to a singular letter per year.

He elected to ignore the wristlet until it buzzed again five minutes later, projecting a confirmation of the letter's completed decontamination.

Agust grumbled but detoured to the distribution facility on his way home. If it was a glitch, the mailbot could fix the wristlet. But instead of hearing Agust's complaint, the mailbot produced another envelope, this one brighter than the other and rivaling the blue of the sky.

It was heavy in his hands. Once home, it seemed to stare him down.

It wasn't often Agust felt fear. He'd spent his twenty years post-graduation cultivating an ecosystem of success for his law firm. He'd signed the documents confirming his family's need for quarantine. He regularly looked murderers in the eye and argued them into submission. Yet now, the simplicity of a cerulean envelope was activating his fight-or-flight response.

Agust chose fight, but not before digging a full head mask and a pair of gloves out of his closet, leftover from his first discovery of his family's infection.

This letter had more burnouts than the previous day's, weaving over cursive handwriting like a maze. Nothing alarming. It was stuffy in the mask, so Agust pulled it off his head, set it on the counter, and resumed his reading, only to be met with another photograph leaping from the pages.

He jumped away. Maybe he would be choosing flight.

The papers fluttered to the floor. Before Agust could replace his mask, he caught a glimpse of the image and froze. He knew this photo. He remembered the day it was taken. He had his own projection disk of it tucked into a containment unit at the bottom of a trunk, along with dozens of other family mementos and heirlooms that he never looked at due to the risk of infection. He was too weak to forget them or throw them away.

The photo showed a younger version of him with his sister. The latter's face bore the faintest hint of the smile that he would later condemn as a symptom of the Disease clawing its way into the open. Agust remembered his copy displaying them in black and white, but this image was so full of color, he could almost taste it. Her dress was lavender, the river behind them elderberry, their eyes basil, and everything saturated beyond his current reality.

The memory flooded Agust's mind. His sister's insistence on going out despite the cold. The warmth of the hot chocolate they'd purchased. The incessant shivering that led to them chasing patches of warm sunlight as their cheeks and noses turned pink.

Agust smiled.

The air against his teeth felt foreign. In the next instant, he ran to the bathroom and stared at the dark eyes of his reflection. No smile. No skin irregularities. Nothing growing out of his forehead. His hands shook as he pried his lips apart and examined his teeth. They were clean white, but he wasn't sure if that indicated health or infection. With a sigh that felt like it rattled his ribs, Agust popped a cleansing tablet into his mouth and wished for it to wash his mind as well.

o

The train is now circling the Earth
Moon. Time until arrival is seven hours.

o

"MISTER CYR. I THOUGHT YOU ALREADY HAD YOUR monthly inspection."

Two days ago, Agust opened his eyes to see his dentist, Dr. Nemanjo, organizing the dental tools. There was no other greeting or eye contact from the man whose hair was as white as the examination room. The doctor was there to do his job in silence apart from the buzzing of the liquid latex machine coating his hands. This bedside manner was one of the reasons Agust preferred Dr. Nemanjo, although another dentist wasn't an option anyway due to the strict assignments in place for control of the Disease.

"I came on the first of the month," Agust confirmed.

"What brings you in again?"

Agust didn't want to be packed up and shipped to Mars automatically, especially with the serial-killing grocerbot case on his work desk, so he explained as vaguely as he could about the colorful envelopes and photographs. He emphasized the assurance of their thorough decontamination from the mailbots and his use of the gloves and the mask. He kept his voice as stoic as possible, as though he were in a courtroom. Only, this time, he was arguing for his own livelihood.

Dr. Nemanjo nodded and sat beside his patient. "There's no problem with caution when it comes to the Disease."

The doctor began his inspection. No tooth or gap was left untouched. A black light ran over Agust's mouth before the doctor stood thirty minutes later. There was no commentary. No small talk. No storytelling. Agust preferred it that way.

Instead, Dr. Nemanjo cracked his knuckles and began to rinse the spray-latex off. He opened the projector on his wristlet, made some notes, and left with two words.

"You're clean."

○

The crew will begin distributing refreshments momentarily. Please return to your seat for the convenience of the staff.

○

AGUST'S WRISTLET BUZZED AGAIN BEFORE HE LEFT the dental facility. He felt the smile before it came and bit his cheeks to keep it at bay. The thought of another letter made him happy, despite the contamination he had to be experiencing. Blood touched his tastebuds when he finally stepped onto the moving sidewalk toward the distribution facility.

As he rode along, Agust's mind took its own path. It had been easy to follow the guidance of the studies when this all started. The research showed the danger in those who smiled or laughed. The rapid death rates. It all seemed reasonable. Factual. The data supported the hypothesis. When nothing was done and his family dismissed the research, Agust had been as frustrated as his peers at the lack of action in the public sector. His sister had once said he lacked nuance. He had called her worldview rose-colored.

The worldwide election that placed the researchers in power was swift. No one wanted premature deaths. In just a month, the world's color was drained or burned. The infected ones were sent to a place where they could live in peace until they died, and their healthy loved ones would not have to watch them succumb.

All the precautions were in place, yet Agust was here, now showing symptoms. He knew that. Something should have concerned Dr. Nemanjo. The confirmation of health with no concern or note made Agust wonder how the diagnosis of his friends and family had been reached. He considered if this research that led to fighting against the Disease had been used in an intentional strategy, whether as reason to colonize Mars or something else.

Agust quickly shook that conspiracy theory from his head and forced himself to avoid thinking of it more after he picked up the letter and returned home. He didn't bother with the mask or gloves.

Today's envelope was the color of a canary. Agust didn't take time to appreciate it, instead letting it fall to the floor. This letter had as many censor burns as the others. Agust didn't care. He scanned lines and flipped pages, eager for another photograph.

He didn't understand why he wanted another. His mind was screaming to throw it all away and inform the mailbots that he no longer wished to accept any mail from the MQC. But Dr. Nemanjo's attitude and the buzz Agust had from the symptomatic smiles made him want another picture. Need it. This had become his obsession and addiction, his latest case, and he never stepped away from a trial until he revealed the truth.

Desperation clawed at his chest when he was presented with another photograph.

The image was ridiculous. It showed the red dust of Mars, a starscape beyond the colony's biodome, and his sister lying on the ground without concern for the white jumpsuit she wore. Her arms and legs were splayed, her grin as wide as a skyway's air-lanes. In the dust was a silhouette Agust had long forgotten: wings, a head, and a skirt, creating the shadow of a scarlet snow angel.

His sister had always loved doing that.

Before he knew what was happening, Agust smiled. Grinned. And laughed.

The noise was strange to his ears. It was as though he were underwater, hearing the noise come from an unknown horizon above him. The only evidence that it was his own laugh was a vibration in his chest that made him wonder if his heart would explode. He laughed all the way to the bathroom, where even his reflection couldn't stop the joyous sound. His face turned pink, bright as one of his sister's envelopes. For a moment, he caught a glint of blue in his eyes. His sides began to ache, and, worst of all, he liked it.

Agust was sick. He knew it. Irrefutably infected, and he didn't care to stop it.

○

The space train is now traveling through a minor asteroid field. Turbulence expected. Please fasten your seatbelts.

○

ONE DAY AGO, HE RETURNED TO THE EXAMINATION room of Dr. Nemanjo's dental facility. The visit was futile, but Agust forced himself to go anyway. His ride on the sidewalk was bathed in the early beams of sunlight, and he had to stop himself from smiling at two blue jays that rode the morning breeze over his head. A tall man ahead of him had to dodge hanging oak branches while scrolling through wristlet projections, causing Agust to disguise his chuckles as coughs.

The Disease was coursing through his veins. His smiles made him a menace to society, yet he roamed free with no one wise to the danger his presence caused. To the best of the authorities' knowledge, he was uncontaminated. If he wanted to, he could turn around at any moment and go home, live out his days under the pretension of health until the tests finally betrayed him. Instead, he kept on his path. Agust didn't know why, but he needed the official diagnosis. He needed to see his identification log marked with the infection symbol to cement the truth, despite knowing it would earn him a ticket to the MQC and finalize this as his last hour on Earth.

Dr. Nemanjo entered as silently as the day before. Before the man could reach his tools, he was stopped by Agust's newfound smile and greeting.

The air seemed to freeze. Agust forced his face into a frown.

If the doctor was afraid, the man didn't indicate it. Instead, he strapped on his mask, buckled it around his neck, and once again applied liquid latex to his hands. The contraption made him look like an old drawing Agust once saw of the extinct orangutan: small holes for eyes, a circle around the muzzle for breathing, and whistles that sounded like a waterlogged flute.

Agust chuckled. Dr. Nemanjo had no reaction.

Once again, Agust's teeth and gums were poked and pulled and prodded and black lit. He shut his eyes and tried to focus on the mechanical smell of the room to distract himself from the mirth that trickled through his mind and body. His world was slowly revealing joy in every corner. It was deadly, and Agust craved more. If this was what his sister felt, he couldn't blame her for refusing treatment. Perhaps her rose-colored reality was closer to truth than his own.

After what felt like an hour, Dr. Nemanjo spoke. "You should come back tomorrow for a follow-up."

Agust didn't need to be told that it wasn't a suggestion.

o

We are now approaching the Mars Quarantine Colony. Remain seated for landing.

o

THE QUARANTINEBOTS SPOTTED AGUST BEFORE HE was within twenty feet of the dental facility. In a nanosecond, they swarmed, secured a perimeter, and locked his arms behind his back, scurrying as though they were dancing to the music of their metronomic beeping.

Agust should have been terrified. He felt his adrenaline surge, much like the day he received the second photo, but this time he didn't choose to fight or to flee. Instead, he smiled and shook his head at the striped bots and their frenzy that made them look like the bees that once flitted through his mother's garden. He wondered if she had one in the MQC. It had been too long since he'd heard from her.

They pushed him into a clear, sealed box. He'd seen these before and always averted his gaze from the humans inside. Infection had been said to be strong enough to pass through not just ideas or physical substances but eyes as well. He wondered if he'd be treated the same by the yet-uninfected. Agust supposed he deserved it.

The bots opened their own projectors, made a few swift motions, and the box rose to float over the ground.

As they turned the box to move him, Agust glanced back at the facility and caught sight of Dr. Nemanjo in the window. For a moment, Agust thought he was in a drug-induced dream. The doctor's face lifted in a smile. There was a brief nod before the dentist's face dropped, and he vanished from the window.

People stared at the procession of bots and their captive. Others covered their eyes or noses. Agust was surprised at the pity he felt, not for himself being led to quarantine but for his repulsed audience. He should have felt sadness. Mourning. Something. His firm would be sold to someone else, his apartment wiped and decontaminated, his belongings burned, and yet Agust couldn't create an ounce of sorrow.

The sky shone with fingertips of golden sunlight tracing over fuchsia clouds that played hide-and-seek among the gray skyscrapers. Agust looked to the bots and his onlookers, tapping his fingers on the glass in reminiscence of a skill long ignored. He wanted to find the same colors in the world around him. There ought to have been green grass or purple flowers, but any beginning sprouts of fauna were all gray.

The procession turned a corner, and Agust saw them. A pair of bright green eyes in the face of a small girl staring up at him, her head tilted in curiosity. He offered a smile. She reached a tiny hand toward him and might have brushed his containment pod if a woman even taller than the quarantine bots hadn't scooped her up.

Agust sighed. The girl reminded him of his sister.

His heart palpitated as he recalled that he'd be seeing her and his parents in mere hours. It had been years. He hoped he would recognize her. That she would recognize him. And even though she clearly held no ill opinions of him, considering the regularity of her letters across their time apart, he couldn't help the lingering thought that she would refuse to see him, and he would somehow be more alone than he was on Earth, with no relatives near him at all.

o

We have successfully docked at the
Mars Quarantine Colony Station.
Please exit to the right.

o

"YOU COMING, HON?"

A crew member interrupted Agust's mental review of his final days on Earth and pulled his mind back onto the train. Though she looked elderly, her stance suggested otherwise. Like the other crew members, she wore no mask, suit, or any other form of safety gear to shield her against the Disease.

Agust looked around and realized he was alone in the galactic train car. The ride itself had been filled with chatter and songs and dancing from his fellow passengers, which he'd opted to remain distant from even when his fingers started itching to tap along with the rhythm. Seeing the car empty and the wide view of space beyond the windows made him feel smaller than a mustard seed.

He stood and cleared his throat. "I don't have a choice, do I?"

She gave him a smile that hinted at as many stories as the Milky Way itself might hold. "I think you've already made yours."

He exited onto a platform with a view of the stars above. More crew members wandered about, none giving him a glance of concern. After following several signs with arrows and having his wristlet scanned by a small identification-bot, he was released through a pair of white doors.

Color assaulted his senses. All the stories of the red planet failed to communicate the true pigmentation of the ground, highlighted by the glow of surrounding lamps. The biodome overhead was clear, allowing for a full panorama of the night sky. Agust wondered if there really were more stars visible here or if he'd just never bothered to look up at them long enough on Earth.

The buildings featured murals and carvings, giving each structure its own identity, in contrast to the gray columns of Earth. Projections advertised new performances and exhibitions at halls with names Agust didn't recognize. The tones of an electronic orchestra drifted from somewhere ahead.

Agust wondered if this whole time he'd been the one quarantined on Earth.

"Agust!"

It was her.

"Elexia?" Agust spoke his sister's name for the first time in ten years.

She ran up from his right, clothed in a bright yellow jumpsuit with matching flowers painted over her face. She didn't look sick. She wasn't dying. Elexia was bright as the sun, and she was beautiful.

In an instant, they embraced.

"I thought you'd never get here," she said.

"I'm too stubborn," he replied. "You know that."

Elexia's laughter rang like a bell, and he joined her.

"It's opening night for Mother and Father," she explained as they separated. "They're in a play together. But I wanted to be here to meet you when you came, whenever you came."

Agust didn't know how many days Elexia and his family must have been waiting for him. He doubted he would've had the same confidence to meet the train every day. The thought made his eyes begin to water.

"Thank you," Agust said.

"Why?"

"For not giving up on me."

She smiled. "I never would. And I never will."

They wandered toward the city and its colors. Smiles met them as they passed their quarantine fellows, waves and greetings flowing gently. Despite being humans in a galactic terrarium, the air somehow was fresh and even floral as they passed intricate pots and arranged plants. They passed a food stand that billowed steam and smelled of coffee. Agust made a mental note to try it sometime.

The music grew louder, and Agust felt his fingers twitch in reply. He wanted to do more than simply listen to music. The notes were crawling inside him. It was a feeling he barely recognized, and he wondered if he would even remember his passion.

"Elexia?"

"Hmm?"

"I ..." Agust struggled to mold his thoughts. "I'd like to play something. On a piano."

He didn't think a smile could be that wide. Once again, Elexia proved him wrong about something.

"There's one in my home. I've been saving it for you."

And now his smile matched hers. The lights and colors were no longer terrifying. The laughter around them was a victory cry.

He was home.

HOLLOW CONSTELLATIONS - BY JUSTIN SANGERMANO

FOR THE FIRST TIME IN FIFTY YEARS, I OPENED MY EYES. THE OVERHEAD LIGHTS OF THE SPACEGOD SHUTTLE BLINDED ME, AND I BLINKED, WAITING FOR my eyes to adjust. I had half expected—no, hoped— to be in bed with my wife, comfortably waking up on a Saturday morning. Instead, I was lying in a metal cryogenic pod. The only sign of Annabelle or our daughter was the picture taped to the pod window. The three of us were on a fishing boat in the photo, and below it was a message from my wife written in Sharpie: "We love you, Klein, aka our Rocket Man!" Seeing this photo brought to mind the memories I'd missed: wedding anniversaries, family vacations, graduations, maybe even the birth of my grandchildren. Thanks to cryogenic sleep, my body hadn't aged much since that photograph was taken, but that was a luxury not given to Anabelle or Claire.

Regret flooded my heart, but it was too late to reverse my dedication to science and humanity.

My daughter and her kids still needed a new planet, I reminded myself, as I found the strength to peel the wires and restraints from my body. The lid pushed open easily, and I floated into the air. It felt like I'd only slept for one night, but I'd just spent over half my life cryogenically frozen. Even as a man of science, I found it hard to fully wrap my head around that. This room of the spacecraft was lined with a dozen metal pods. They were each the size of a coffin and had the same function: to carry motionless bodies, in this case to the heavens.

Laughter filled the area as we all woke up and floated around. "I feel like Superman," said Ian, a tech expert I'd grown close to over the years of training for this mission. He imitated flying with his arm extended until he reached the door before spinning its wheel and opening it.

One by one, we drifted out of the room and into the hall, making various jokes like, "How did you sleep?" and "I feel like I haven't seen you in fifty years." Every wall, ceiling, and floor in the SpaceGod shuttle was home to some wire or piece of tech, each individually labeled. While a bit unsightly, the wires had to be accessible in an emergency; you don't want to be yanking picture frames and decorations off the walls to locate an electrical fire while drifting through the cosmos.

Justin Sangermano

I wafted toward the window and stared out at space for the first time. I'd been frozen right after takeoff, unable to gaze at the stars, but now I was awestruck by them. It was like staring out at a valley from a mountaintop and being able to see through the trees. An area of space around the back of the ship was blurred as the space-time was expanded. My work had been crucial in the calculations of altering space-time for our speedy travel, which guaranteed me a spot on the crew. It wouldn't be fair to call myself *the* brains of the operation, though; even the crewmember with the lowest IQ still scored higher than Einstein. Other geniuses on board had made discoveries that were thought possible only in science fiction, such as the means for our suspended animation and the prevention of muscle atrophy. All of our minds played a crucial role in this mission. Not to mention our physicality. The gravity of the new world was twice as strong as Earth's, so a robust crew would be needed even for tasks we'd think of as minor physical labor on Earth.

From the outside, the SpaceGod shuttle looked like an overstuffed plane. It landed vertically but flew horizontally. It had three fins at its base that both controlled the rocket's direction and functioned as landing gear. The cockpit, which was as big as some apartments on Earth, was visible from the giant window in the front of the shuttle's nose. Smaller windows ran along the spacecraft's back like spots on a leopard.

I performed aerial somersaults until I saw our leaders, Godrick Cullen Jr., the son of SpaceGod's founder, and Angelica Keb, a former military general. The co-captains had been frozen in a different section of the ship in case complications occurred, as had the additional five hundred civilians we kept below deck for future repopulation efforts. My family would have been part of this group had Anabelle not decided her medical career on Earth was too much to sacrifice.

We saluted our captains. The time for fun and jokes had ended. "At ease," Captain Keb said. Her neatly tied brunette ponytail was the opposite of bedhead, with not a hair out of place despite the fact that she'd spent the last fifty years asleep. "We're set to reach the black hole in twenty-two Earth hours. Get to your stations and get ready."

"Remember to grab your watches by the door on your way," Captain Cullen said. The only hair on his head was a reddish goatee. "They'll be synced together according to the time it was on Earth when we left. And, by the way, welcome back to the world of the awakened."

o

"SO DID YOU HAVE ANY DREAMS WHILE YOU WERE out?" my fellow scientist Gemma asked me. She was tossing up a pen and letting it hover ever higher.

I stared at a metal mechanism in front of us. To the untrained eye, it looked like a simple metal tube, but I saw it for the miraculous invention it was. It was responsible for the alteration in space-time that made our faster-than-light space travel possible.

My eyes didn't move from the machine; I couldn't allow myself to get distracted. "I don't think that's scientifically possible, doctor."

"I guess not," she said. "Still, though, it would've been nice to have something going on up there during all those lost years, don't you think?"

"We're all gonna lose several more years if we don't get these calculations right."

"I'm sorry."

Gemma had a beautiful mind but was easily sidetracked. This was not the time to divert focus. According to my estimates, there was about a 50 percent chance we would successfully make it through the black hole into the next galaxy, and an equal chance the extreme gravitational pull would destroy our ship and everyone in it. All precautions up until this point had been taken to ensure we got this right. It felt like we'd run thousands of simulations to find the proper speed for our ship and the right duration of our suspended animation.

Gemma left her pen adrift as she joined me to stare at the machine, biting her fingernail like she always did when she was deep in thought. In a matter of minutes, she verified the calculations and assured me that with only a slight curve to the right, we would be en route to the center of the black hole's singularity and would not be "turned into pasta noodles." This was why I liked working with Gemma; her mind worked faster than mine, both with science and jokes.

"I hope I dream tonight," she said, carrying on our previous conversation, which I had already disregarded.

"How come?"

"I wanna see Earth one more time, don't you?"

I tried in vain to stop my thoughts from turning to the family I had left behind. "Earth's behind us now." I submitted our completed work to the captains before adding, "Thanks for your help, doctor."

o

AFTER THREE HOURS OF LABORIOUS WORK AT OUR designated posts, the crew took a break in the mess hall, discussing various topics over ice cream, or at least what they called ice cream. It came in chalklike chunks in a bag and could be eaten with your fingers. I, however, sat alone in the corner of the room behind a computer screen, attempting to call my family. I tried and tried, but the call would not go through. Feeling my technical age of eighty-seven, I summoned Ian to help me. I'm a smart guy, don't get me wrong, but I'm physics-smart, not tech-smart. They're different. Ian took another bite of ice cream as he drifted over. I watched as he replicated the exact procedure I had done with the same results.

"That's weird," he muttered.

"Has this happened to anyone else?" I asked.

"Pretty sure most of us were waiting to start families until we're in the next world. As far as I know, you're the first one to try to contact Earth." He poked his head up from the monitor and called to the crew, "Hey, has anyone tried to phone home?"

Everyone shook their heads.

"Nope, you're the first one."

"I see that. Why do you think it won't go through?"

"I'm not sure. Let me check something." He exited the application and ran a new program that displayed two parallel lines that both contained two spikes. A ball traveled along each line, gaining speed at the peaks. They resembled the heart monitors used in old hospitals.

"What are you doing?" I asked.

"Checking something."

We were silent for a minute while the program displayed numbers I did not understand. I took a deep breath through my nose, still unused to the lack of scent. The metallic odor of space could only be smelled in the airlock after space walks (or so I'd been told—we had not yet done a space walk), but the odor of astronauts who couldn't shower would surely build up in this spacecraft without the ability to open a window. Maybe the present lack of scent was a blessing.

"The message request is being sent, but it's not being accepted by anything."

"So Earth is blocking the signal?"

"Not exactly. There doesn't seem to be anything blocking it, it's just not being accepted."

"Wait, so what does—"

The commanding voice of Captain Keb axed my words like a lumberjack. "Is everything okay?"

When had she appeared behind us? How long had she been watching?

"Yeah," said Ian. "I was just wondering, can we contact our families before we arrive in Goppith?"

"I thought you never married?" Captain Keb asked.

"I didn't," said Ian, "but I still got a mother, right?"

"It's been fifty years, Dr. Hlass. I wouldn't count on it." She cleared her throat and called to the entire crew, "Break time is over. Everyone, get back to your stations." She refocused her attention on Ian and me. "We have too much to focus on for flowery conversations and recaps of Earth news. There will be plenty of time for chitchat when we've arrived safely in our new home."

As she floated away, Ian turned toward me and mouthed an insult at her expense. "Don't worry, Klein, I'm gonna look into this. Just give me some time."

"I promised my family I'd call them," I said. "I have to hear Claire's laugh again. It's been fifty years, damn it! Anabelle is gonna be worried sick if she's still ali—"

I coughed as if I'd inhaled smoke. I'd never admitted the terrible truth out loud.

"Sorry, I just— I don't want to hear about my loved ones' deaths secondhand. The sooner I get on those phones, the sooner I'm a part of their lives again."

But was I ever a part of their lives? Wasn't I always in the lab or buried in some study? I was almost thankful for the fifty-year pause in my thoughts, because it meant relief from a specific guilt I'd been carrying for years. They say being in space makes your problems feel small, but even among the stars, I bore the guilt for missing parent day at Claire's school fifty-one years ago. I had no excuse. I overworked and missed it. I was supposed to present a replica of the SpaceGod shuttle to her grade school class, but I never showed. It's a shameful fact that this was a trend for me. Even when I was on Earth, I was hardly there. And now my daughter had seen more years of life than I. If she were alive, could I blame her if she didn't want to see me?

Ian clapped me on the back in a friendly manner. "I'll do everything I can, but this isn't going to be a quick fix. Especially not with the captains looking over our shoulders. Let's get to work and keep their eyes off us. Oh, and you should grab a bag of that ice cream before it's gone, Klein. Maybe this is just my fifty years of not eating talking, but that stuff is a gourmet feast."

I stretched my arms as I moved away from the screen. After sleeping for half a century, I was still exhausted. "Thanks. I guess you're right."

He smiled. "Always am."

o

IAN STILL HAD NO LUCK AS WE NEARED THE BLACK hole. Our captains and pilots in the cockpit were the only ones who could do anything to help us now, so I forced myself to be content watching the window in front of me as I was strapped into a chair with the rest of the crew surrounding me. As we entered the black hole, it went completely dark, blacking out the balls of flame that had been scattered in the distance as if the window itself had been covered by a blanket.

In this eerie moment, I felt closer to death than I ever had before. I closed my eyes and thought of my wife. Annabelle was thirty-seven when I left the planet; we both were, but I was the only one who remained this age. Eighty-seven wasn't an unlikely age to live past, and she had always been in good health, but accidents do occur. If her automated car had led her to a crash or the house had erupted in flames, I wondered if her soul would be floating through the very space I was traveling in. I never was one for religion, but at this moment, I prayed the black hole was heaven and I would see my wife again if a tragedy had befallen her.

Suddenly, a scorching heat took hold of the room as if we had flown through the sun. I began to wonder if this was hell. I thought I felt myself stretching, something I knew might happen. My daughter, Claire, always said I was tall, but now I would be even taller. She would be a grown woman by now, and I wondered which of us would be taller when we reconnected.

"We made it," a crew member called.

This was met with thunderous applause. The room cooled down tremendously, and I opened my eyes to see a slightly taller crew and stars dotting the sky once more. No angelic presence would greet us. I was alive but somehow disappointed.

°

"DO YOU EVER WONDER IF THERE'S MORE TO THIS mission than we're being told?" Ian asked me during dinner that evening.

I nearly choked on a dehydrated carrot. "No."

We weren't alone in the mess hall—astronauts floated all around us. This was not the kind of talk others needed to hear; conspiracy theories aren't fun to think about while floating through an endless vacuum of stars and rocks.

Ian leaned in closer and whispered, "Based on everything I've seen, the captains know way more about this mission than we do."

"I mean, yeah, that's typically how things work in a chain of command."

"But we don't even know the true purpose of this mission. There's something they aren't telling us."

"And you know this how?"

"I have no proof."

"Well, there you go."

"Which is why you're gonna help me get it."

I sighed and ran my hands through my hair. Without gravity, it stood exactly as I ruffled it. "Ian, all I wanted was to talk to my family. We have enough going on with finding humanity's new home, we don't need to add—"

Ian shushed me and looked over both shoulders before continuing softly, "After you couldn't make that call, I started poking around in the ship's database. That's where I found a file encrypted heavier than anything I've ever seen. It's got tighter security than the government's nuclear system."

"How do you know that?"

"I hacked the software in college to see if I could," Ian said. "Please don't tell anyone that. It's highly confidential, but also probably the main reason they knew I was qualified for this mission. Anyways— look, if you can get close to Captain Cullen in the next few hours, I can get the cameras offline while you snag his key card—"

"Wait, his what?"

"With his key card, I can bypass the first step in accessing his log. There will still be some heavy decrypting, but that'll only take me a couple of hours … I think."

"How do you expect me to get the captain's key card?" I asked. "It's literally attached to his hip. Not to mention that every inch of this ship is under constant surveillance."

"I'll get the cameras offline, but you need to distract him. Got any ideas?"

"No."

"All right, let's brainstorm, then."

"Ian, I don't have any ideas because I'm not helping you with this!"

"Do you want to talk to your family again or not?"

When I didn't answer, he pressed further. "Well, this is how you make that call possible."

"You're insane," I said with a sigh of frustration.

"Oh yeah, big time. So let me ask you again: do you have any ideas on how to distract Captain Cullen?"

"I think so," I said without much confidence. "Wish me luck."

○

"IT'S A BRILLIANT IDEA," GEMMA SAID AS WE TRAVELED toward Captain Cullen's quarters. "But I think you should be the one to present it to him. It's your idea, after all."

"Yeah, but you're more of a people person," I urged her. "He's more likely to listen to you."

Gemma accepted this, and we continued. Captain Cullen was right at the door as we approached; he had been expecting us. We entered with his permission, and Gemma handed him the tablet with our presentation on it. It showcased a new strategy in space-time alteration that I had come up with to increase our speed by 20 percent, thus shaving a considerable amount of time off our remaining journey. I had the idea a couple of months ago—well, a couple of months and fifty years ago—but had wanted to test it a few more times before taking it up the ladder. However, I no longer cared if the calculations were precise; their new main purpose was to serve as a distraction, regardless of whether the captains wanted to use them.

The key card was in a retractable badge holder clipped to the captain's belt. It dangled from its cord as Captain Cullen examined the tablet. Floating to his right, I kept my hands at my sides, slowly and discreetly reaching over. Gemma made a joke I missed, and she laughed loudly, giving me the perfect time to snatch the keycard and pocket it. But stealing from my captain wasn't my area of expertise, so my nerves let that golden opportunity slip by.

"I like this idea," Captain Cullen said when the presentation concluded, "but let me talk it over with Captain Keb before I give you a definitive answer."

He held the tablet out. Although Gemma was closer to him, I had to be the one to grab it from him. I kicked off the wall and, like a rowdy child in the pool, floated toward him with enough speed to crash into him. I put my hands on his back and waist as if to steady myself. My left hand wrapped around the card in its holder.

"Oops, sorry, sir. Still getting used to the lack of gravity," I lied.

I slid my hand away as if innocently removing myself from an accidental collision. But as my hand rose, it slid the key card up with it, unclipping the holder from his waist. I grabbed the tablet from him with the other hand and smiled with relief as I floated back out his door.

o

THE DECRYPTING TOOK IAN LONGER THAN HE HAD predicted, and several concerns began to arise. For one, I had to report to the science room to run tests in an hour. If I wasn't there, Gemma might come looking for me. Also, we had tried to discreetly discard Captain Cullen's card after we were through with it in the hope that he would find it floating somewhere and think himself responsible, but I secretly doubted the strength of this plan. Lastly, Ian had rigged the camera in this room to show a previous hour, and that loop had repeated at least twice. If the captains hadn't noticed that by now, it wasn't likely to take them much longer.

"Ah-ha!" Ian finally exclaimed, which only mildly calmed my anxiety. "Ready to see what our flawless captains have been hiding?"

"Just get me in contact with my wife, and I'll love you forever."

"Attaboy." Ian opened the file labeled 'GAFORK_ MEETING.'

A video began to play. It was an overhead view—most likely from a security camera on the ceiling—of a meeting in an official-looking room. A well-groomed man with an expensive blue suit sat on one side of the table. I recognized him as the mastermind behind our trek; it was the late Godrick Cullen Sr., founder of SpaceGod and father of Captain Cullen. Given his relatively healthy appearance, the video had to be from almost a century ago, but the SpaceGod

CEO had aged so much in his final years that it was hard to judge the time gap based on his appearance alone.

Ian paused the video when he saw what Cullen Sr. was talking to. "Is that what I think it is?" he asked.

The being at the other end of the table had eight rocky tentacles and stood on five of them. It was covered with a thick, creamy slime that slid off its red exterior and onto the tan carpet. After a moment of scientific fascination, I reminded myself that the confirmation of extraterrestrial life wouldn't help me reach my daughter, so I resumed the video.

Godrick Cullen Sr. introduced himself, and a flat machine on the oval table, presumably a translator, made clicking sounds to the alien. Their guest spoke in a similar set of clicks in a voice resembling a high-pitched frog's croak. The translator conveyed its greetings: its name was General Gafork of the planet Wasajed, and it had an offer for Earth.

"Have you ever heard of that planet?" I asked Ian.

He shook his head. "I've never seen an alien before, either."

"I'll hear your deal," said Godrick Cullen Sr. in the video. "But for my carpet's sake, make it quick."

I still wonder if the translator included that last part.

The alien spoke again, and the machine translated its words. "Mr. Cullen, my people have been watching your career with great interest for quite some time.

We admire that someone in such a primitive species can even comprehend space travel like you do. Your rockets and technology are far beyond what was thought to be possible in your world. Your mission to colonize a new planet is honorable, and with just a little assistance from Wasajed, it's entirely possible for you to accomplish."

"You traveled all these light-years just to buy stock in my company?" Cullen Sr. asked.

"My home world's contribution to SpaceGod is only the first step in our deal," said the alien general. "It is merely the catalyst to ensure that your technology is sufficiently advanced for this plan's success.

"You see, Mr. Cullen, Earth has blown through its resources and is clearly at the end of its time. Despite oceans covering three-quarters of your planet, the water that your population can actually drink won't sustain it for much longer. My species does not require water as heavily as humans do. We have evolved differently. We have conquered several other worlds, one of which is perfect for earthlings. There are plenty of resources, water included, and no species higher up on the evolutionary timeline, meaning a lack of notable predators. You've been looking for a planet to terraform. This wouldn't even require that."

"Sounds too good to be true. What do you want in return?"

"Like Earth, my planets are dying. Seven hundred years ago, the atmosphere and climate of my home planet, Wasajed, were destroyed seemingly beyond repair—until my ancestors built a lifesaving machine. It stabilized our planet's atmosphere and climate. It even doubled our natural resources. Since then, we've replicated these machines to continue feeding the planets of our empire, but we have run into a problem: a lack of energy to sustain them. The energy we require can only be found on planets like Earth."

"If this is about oil, you'll have to take it up with the—"

"Not oil. Our resource can only be created from humans."

"Wait, what the hell?" I said, way louder than I meant to—I practically shouted it.

Cullen Sr. looked as dumbstruck in the video as I felt watching it. "Come again?" he asked.

The machine translated for the alien, "At the time of death, a human's soul gives off an energy that is unlike the energy produced by any other creature across the universe. We can harvest this energy. By collecting the life force of eight billion human souls, we can jump-start the machines we need to save our empire."

Ian and I swore under our breath but didn't dare talk over the recording.

"I don't know how things work on your planet," Cullen Sr. growled, "but here on Earth, we don't just let *one* person sign away an entire planet! I'm tired of this absurd deal already. Get out of my—"

"Why must anyone know about this deal?"

"How the fuck would I keep it a secret?"

"Your company has been working on a mission to the stars for years, as we discussed. This fact is known to every human on your planet, even if many laugh at your intergalactic travel efforts. So we'll help you finish your rocket and send you to our planet while the rest of your decaying world believes you acted alone and are simply scouting for potential planets to live on."

"You expect the people of Earth to believe that our government poured millions into my research just to send a ship on a simple scouting mission? We'd never do it like that! I'd only send boots out of the atmosphere if I was absolutely sure that we had found a planet—"

"So say you are colonizing another world. Your fans will praise you for it, and the naysayers will assume you will fail. I care not for the specifics of what you tell your people in search of their approval."

"Leaders all over the world will come after me for this!"

"Not if they never know this meeting took place. All I need is one human being's approval—mainly to abide by my home world's procedures and guidelines—and then we can send a fleet of flying saucers to your world and harvest all the souls after you've already left."

Ian hurled a vulgar insult at the screen like I used to during televised ball games.

"Would it be painful?" Cullen Sr. asked. "The harvesting process, I mean."

More clicking. "Do you really want to know?"

Cullen Sr. groaned. "Doesn't matter. Painful or not, what if I'm not willing to sacrifice the lives of several billion human beings?"

"Then save your planet before it hits the breaking point. You don't have much time before Earth goes the way of Wasajed, but there is still time to make an impact."

"How am I supposed to stop it? I'm a businessman, not a goddamn miracle worker!"

Even though the video quality wasn't high definition, I could see the sweat dripping down Cullen Sr.'s face. The man seemed to be searching for a higher authority, but he was the richest man on Earth. If the alien was running off the cliché of "Take me to your leader," then it had come to the right man, going strictly off wealth.

"Is that your final answer, Mr. Cullen?"

Ian and I both stirred in the silence awaiting Cullen Sr.'s decision. Who knew about this? Did the businessman even tell his son?

The alien pressed further. "By our predictions, life will end on Earth either way. I see the lack of some resources, the abundance of others, and your people's inability to share all of them. Your species has doomed itself to a fiery end. With my solution, you can ensure that a select group of your species survives with an abundance of all resources. It will be a new beginning."

Godrick Cullen Sr. didn't look like he'd accept the deal. He sat still for so long that Ian even checked the screen to make sure the video had not frozen. It had not. The SpaceGod CEO was just deep in thought.

"Your planet isn't the only thing that's dying," said the alien.

Godrick Cullen Sr. scoffed. "You saw that quicker than my doctor did."

"The hell?" Ian muttered. "That *thing* can screen for cancer?"

I shushed him and leaned closer to the video. The translator was conveying the alien's words.

"You may not live to see the next stage of humanity, but you'll be remembered as a hero. Does your planet have those?"

"None that I believe in." Godrick Cullen Sr.'s words were hardly audible in the footage.

"Then you could be the first. Your name will be remembered as the one who found humanity's new home. You will have saved everyone on Earth."

"I will have handed them to you."

"But the next generation of humans won't know that. You alone will hold the pen that writes your legacy. If you choose, you'll be remembered as a pioneer and a trailblazer. Who would question it?

All your naysayers will be left on Earth to power our machines."

"All right. I accept."

My watch buzzed, alerting me that I was due at my post. Ian paused the video on an image of Cullen Sr. refusing to shake the alien's tentacle.

"If this is true," I said, "then we need to let the people of Earth know. My family is still on that planet, and I cannot let them die."

Denial is a funny thing; you only realize you were in it when you've been crushed by acceptance or anger.

"Who do we tell?" Ian asked. "If the richest man on Earth already agreed to this, then who's supposed to stop it?"

"I don't know," I mumbled. "Let's agree right now: we keep looking into this but continue doing our jobs in the meantime so it doesn't look like anything is off."

"I agree," Ian said. "You go to your post, and I'll go back to my post. We'll talk about this later, yeah?"

"Yeah," I whispered. "Yeah."

○

GEMMA AND I WERE IN THE LAB RUNNING THE calculations for a dark matter pickup, but we couldn't work at our normal pace. I was usually the one to keep us on track, but I was even more distracted than she was. She went on about unrelated topics—

something about how she hoped the new world would have steak—but I hardly took any of it in.

All my sacrifices ... what were they for? I left everything and everyone in my life for the betterment of society, not realizing that they were the literal sacrifices needed for this mission.

"You motion sick or something?" Gemma asked me. "You look like you're gonna puke."

I shook my head, but she didn't look convinced.

"How long do you think the puke would float here before we could fling it into space?" she wondered aloud.

I was relieved when Captain Cullen's voice came on the room's intercom asking me to meet him in his quarters—until I realized there was only one thing he could want to talk to me about.

o

"ENTER," CAPTAIN GODRICK CULLEN JR. SAID AS I knocked on his door. I wasn't surprised to find Captain Keb accompanying him. "Dr. Redman, I've been looking over your and Gemma's recommendations for space-time modifications, and I must say I'm impressed. But, unfortunately, that's not what I brought you in here to talk about."

The window on the back wall was the biggest in the entire ship, next to the cockpit. Maybe from here, we could see the distant wasteland that used to be Earth. The captains deserved to face that horror outside their window.

"What is it, Captain?" I asked, masking my fear.

"It's Dr. Hlass," Godrick Cullen Jr. said. "He's dead."

My heart fell out of orbit. "Ian? What happened?"

"He was working on a technological issue with the cargo bay door," Captain Keb said. "It wouldn't shut properly, and Dr. Hlass volunteered to fix it."

"He was repairing the panel when it malfunctioned again," Captain Cullen added.

Then Captain Keb ripped off the Band-Aid with, "I'm afraid to report that Ian Hlass was sucked into the vacuum of space. Very tragic."

I had no concrete proof, but I didn't need it. My gut told me the harmonizing captains were lying. There had been no malfunction; it was too convenient.

"I know the two of you were close," Captain Cullen said. "I'm sorry for your loss."

"It's terrible," I mumbled.

A portrait of Godrick Cullen Sr. hung on the wall. It was the only picture on the whole spacecraft. I never thought I'd be thanking cancer, but the disease was the only thing stopping the older Godrick Cullen from being on this ship. His nepo-baby son wasn't much better, but at least he hadn't been the one to sign away the lives of an entire planet.

Captain Keb cleared her throat. "Dr. Redman, it has also come to our attention that the late Dr. Hlass was working on an *unauthorized* project before he died. You wouldn't happen to know anything about this, would you?"

I shook my head. In the sloppiness of my sorrow, I must have let some doubt show on my face.

"You want to contact Earth?" Captain Cullen asked me.

I nodded. "I miss my family."

"I miss mine, too," said Captain Cullen. "Be honest with me, Dr. Redman, and I won't penalize you for anything. Did you see the same video that Dr. Hlass saw?"

I thought about lying, but what was the point? "Yes."

"Well, then you know about the deal and the check my father had to write those aliens," he continued.

I always thought of Captain Keb as the 'bad cop,' and maybe she was, but that didn't make Cullen the 'good cop.' If anything, we just had the 'mean cop' and the 'greedy cop's son.'

"How long do they have?" I asked.

"That check has already been cashed," said Captain Cullen.

"*What?!*" I shouted. "My family? What about—"

"Thank you, Dr. Redman," said Captain Keb with a fake smile.

"*You can't do this!*" I bellowed at my superiors. "My family didn't deserve this—"

"You are dismissed, Klein," said Captain Cullen. "Please keep this conversation private, and don't tell anyone else about Ian's passing until we formally announce it. We just thought you'd want to know first."

"And obviously," Captain Kebb added, "the *rest of it* is classified. Leak that information or even threaten to leak it, and you'll be joining Dr. Hlass in the stars. That'll be all."

○

I LAY STRAPPED DOWN IN MY POD THAT NIGHT, remembering a lesson I had once taught my daughter. I told her that she always had to do the right thing, to take the moral high ground even when the odds were against her. No matter the situation or external pressures, she had to stay true to herself. After everything I had seen and learned, I could not in good conscience continue on this mission knowing what had happened to the people of Earth. If my family was already gone, and their sacrifice along with the rest of the earthlings had helped us secure this deal for humanity's future, then I had to do right by them. But what did that mean?

My previous yearning for religion returned. I didn't believe in a God in the stars, but I would've loved the chance to roll down a shuttle window and ask Him for advice. What would He have me do? Carry on the mission or abort the whole operation?

How the hell would I oppose the mission? Kill the captains and lose all sense of order? Organize a strike? Escape in a pod? Screw that—I'd die within hours, hit by a meteor or a shooting star, or I'd run out of food or air. No, there was nothing I could do, and if I derailed the entire mission with some kind of rebellious attempt, I would be damning humanity. Then the sacrifices of my wife and daughter would all be for nothing. Maybe I could reveal the truth about Ian's death to the rest of the crew when the time was right. But would the time ever be right? Even if I waited until we landed on Goppith, there would still be work to do. Could humanity's next home be built by a crew that resented its leaders? Was it better to take these truths to my grave?

The pods were soundproof, so I screamed until my throat stopped producing noise and my pod became as silent as the space we traveled through. Then I did what I thought was the right thing to do: I let my despair guide me to sleep so I'd be rested for the next day.

In my dreams, I returned to a previous memory. Anabelle sat across from me at our dining room table, a mug of coffee in hand. It was late, and she'd been using the caffeine to stay awake for my arrival. It seemed karmic that after fifty years of not seeing her, this was the conversation I would relive.

"You missed parent day at school today," she told me with clear frustration.

"I'm sorry, I just got held up at the—"

"I know," she said. "I heard it when you missed dinner with my parents, and our anniversary celebration, and my sister's—"

"I know. I can't apologize enough."

"Wouldn't help anyway. Kids at Claire's school are teasing her, y'know? They think she doesn't have a father."

"That's a messed-up thing for them to bully her about."

"They're kids, Klein. Besides, are they wrong?"

She might as well have dumped her hot coffee on my face.

"Come with me to Goppith," I urged her. "I know I've sacrificed too much of our time together on Earth, but it'll all be worth it if you just come with me."

Anabelle shook her head and took another drink. "We've talked about this, Klein. I'm needed at the hospital, and it wouldn't be fair to take Claire out of school where her friends are."

"You *just* said she's being bullied at that school." I took a deep breath; I wasn't trying to worsen this fight. "Annie, please. There's still room on the shuttle, and we'll have more of a future on Goppith than on Earth—"

"*We* don't have a future together. I think we've both known that for a while now. So you go be a Rocket Man, and I'll stay here and raise our daughter."

So far, the dream had played out exactly like the authentic memory. But the tone shifted as a shadow covered the room. When it dissipated, Anabelle was little more than a skeleton. She still drank the coffee, though, and it poured out of her ribcage like a leaky cup.

"Was it worth it?" she asked.

"Was what worth it?" I asked in horror.

"Sacrificing us."

"I didn't sacrifice you—"

"You were complicit in the deal that killed us."

Behind her, I now saw the decaying body of my daughter lying on the kitchen counter like it was a coffin. Tears welled in my dream self's eyes.

"I didn't even know about the deal," I said. "There was nothing I could have done to prevent this."

"Maybe not," Anabelle said. "But you were in the stars when we died. You could have been sitting at this table with us instead, holding our hands until the end, *Rocket Man*."

My eyes snapped open inside the pod. My face was wet; apparently, I'd been crying in real life, too. "It was just a nightmare," I muttered. "She never would have said those things."

I was a hero, I reminded myself, even if I didn't truly believe it. I was forging a new future for humanity. And all of this, I was doing for them, even if their lives had been the price. Humanity had to carry on, and because of me, it would. If I ever get the chance to reconnect with Annabelle and Claire on the spiritual plane, I'll make them understand that my absence from their lives was for the greater good, and so were the sacrifices they didn't know they had to make.

LUNAR BLUES - BY HEIDE R ORLETH

THE DOME LOOKED ITS BEST AT NIGHT. THE DAYTIME SHEER BLUE ILLUSION DROPPED, AND THE STARS CAME OUT TO PLAY, COUNTLESS DROPLETS OF SILVER on a black velvet background. Strips of light lined the walkways that marched out in a perfect grid from the city's center. Selene, the beating heart of humanity's first lunar colony.

Emilio strolled down one of the smaller thoroughfares with his boisterous group, absently nodding along to the girl on his arm, rambling a story about something he couldn't remember. He snapped out of his reverie when they passed a squat storefront on a city block that didn't quite blend in with its glossy, geometric surroundings. It took him a moment to read its neon sign: Tommy's Down-Home Diner.

Emilio realized that he had come to a stop in front of the restaurant's frosted glass door. He wasn't sure as to why. There was nothing remarkable about Tommy's besides its obvious incongruence with the chrome ensconcing it on all sides. It looked more like a relic plucked from the bygone Earth than a carefully planned part of the lunar settlement.

"Emi, what's taking you so long?" the girl asked. He did not know what her name was—Jazz? Casey?— but she didn't matter in the long run. None of that night's group would. He shrugged off her arm and waved the others away without breaking his focus on the diner.

"Go on without me, I'll catch up." None of them acknowledged that there was no way he would find them after they left. Chances were, they would forget he was ever missing by the time the blue sky came back online. Emilio was left alone to ponder why an ordinary diner had so thoroughly seized his attention.

He took a step toward the entrance, reaching a hand to grasp the retro door handle before he aborted the motion. Something in him withered at the thought of opening the door alone, a feeling that made his outstretched hand tremble. After a beat, he smothered the unease, pressed his palm to the metal, and pushed it open with little fanfare, just the tinkling of a bell from somewhere inside.

It was as if he had stepped right into one of those old history simulations. Hues of pastel pink and sky blue bloomed across every surface, diffusing a brightness much warmer than that of the streetlights.

Tinny guitar and gravelly vocals blared from a lovingly restored jukebox opposite the entrance. A long bar counter branched out from the wall, curving around a protruding kitchen. Two of the booths on the wall adjacent to the door were occupied by couples, and the bar was mostly empty save for a half-asleep man in a Maintenance Department jumpsuit sipping a milkshake. Right next to the door was a framed black-and-white picture of the original Tommy's back on Earth, a small plaque underneath dating to 1954—well over a century ago. Where the outside world was cold and impersonal, the inside of the diner was crammed with character. The walls and ceiling were cluttered with old-world memorabilia—event flyers, rusted license plates, a novelty analog clock fashioned like a cartoon cat. Neon lights in pink, blue, and mint green were scattered around, casting everything in a psychedelic glow.

Sure, the window screens sometimes flickered before going on with their regularly scheduled illusions, and the booths were cracked with age, but it felt perfectly natural. The robotic waitstaff rolled along tracks embedded in the checkerboard floor. He watched one deliver food, then roll toward the back of the kitchen, where it stopped, faced the wall, and awaited the next command.

Emilio was alone. He could—should—have sat at the bar, but one booth, three from the end, called to him. He slid across its wrinkled blue vinyl seat, stopping right between two tears so they bracketed his thighs. A new song streamed from the jukebox, one about dreaming of better lives and a future, open wide. He could almost feel the soft kiss to his brow, hear her familiar laugh. A gentle, tentative smile twisted his lips, and he looked up in delight to see—

Nothing. Just an empty bench. Profound disappointment squeezed his lungs tight. He was breathing hard when the android came into view.

"Hey t-t-there," the robot stuttered. "Welcome to Tommy's D-down-Home Diner, E-Emilio Salinas Junior." Emi snapped to attention. Automatic identification was nothing new; it would be impossible to keep a city that relied on life-support systems in an atmosphere-free environment running if there weren't an exact count of its residents. Every person had given up a life on Earth to confine themselves within three pressurized domes with a very rarely changing populace. Buildings like Tommy's were sprinkled among the modernity to nurture nostalgia for what the lunar colonists had left behind. The robot, with its beehive hair and metal dress, carried on.

"Would you like your u-usual order, da-arling?" Now, that caught him off guard. What did it think his usual order was? He couldn't recall ever entering Tommy's before, let alone ordering a specific meal.

"Yes, ma'am, thank you." He wasn't quite sure where the words were coming from, but it felt fitting to say them, right down to the bright smile he gave the android as it rotated on the spot and continued with predictable efficiency. Emilio's eyebrows furrowed as he scanned the dining space.

Five patrons were more than he would have expected for a twenty-four-hour spot in a relatively slow-moving corner of a literal bubble. Though the sun had set hours before, the false windows lining the wall showed a stereotypical view of small-town Americana. A sleepy main street, perhaps during an early autumn afternoon, with leaves the color of burnished bronze everywhere you looked. Emilio was transfixed by the wide sidewalks and vibrant buildings—clear inspirations for Tommy's. He hadn't seen scenery like that since…since…*when*? Something itched at his brain. He could remember walking down one of those streets, his young hand in the grasp of a grown-up's, looking up at—

The image was gone. He shook his head, but whether he was trying to remember the rest or forget it all, he didn't know. The half memory brought pangs of longing and comfort in equal measure, and it took a moment for his uneven breathing to stabilize. He regarded the rest of the room with cautious interest.

The wall his bench faced gave him pause. In numerous eclectic frames—arranged alongside retro movie posters and scenic paintings—were pictures of people. The framed screens cycled through images of what he presumed to be past patrons. People were posed around tables laden with diner food, party supplies, all sporting toothy grins. He saw candid shots of people caught mid-laughter, newly engaged couples, a child blowing out birthday candles with his mother's arms around his shoulders…

The latter captured his attention and stole his breath in one fell swoop. The mother and son had matching dimples, the same loose curls. Her eyes were filled with so much *love* and pride aimed squarely at the boy, whose blinding grin Emilio swore he had seen that day. *But that's impossible, right?* Judging by the background and the pristine condition of the booth, the photo must have been taken ages before, so that kid would be much older, maybe…maybe around Emilio's age. And it must have been taken at *this* Tommy's—he spotted the same android with the beehive updo in the picture's background. But that didn't line up. In an extremely isolated city like theirs, it was easy to know every face, and that kid's smile…he hadn't ever seen it outside of pictures and mirrors.

Wait, what? Mirrors?

"Here you g-go, sweetie. Chocolate chip pancakes and orange juice for Emilio, and eggs B-b-enedict for A-amal-lia, with a side of hashb-browns and c-c-coffee." The robot stuttered through his mother's name, but he had heard enough. He scrambled for his juice and took a long sip to clear his throat. The taste of the citrus piled memories up all around him.

Emi remembered frantically gulping down juice to wash away the bitter tang of coffee while his mother laughed. She had let him take a sip after he pestered and pleaded the way only children can. Her gentle hands had wiped a stray drop from his chin, and she ordered another juice. *Take your time, mijo, there's no rush*, the memory whispered to him.

Shaky hands reached for utensils as the image faded away. His pulse pounded in his ears so loud that he couldn't hear the clatter of his knife against the plate. Emilio shoved a forkful of artificial syrup–soaked pancakes in his mouth to suffocate the lingering citrus. Another memory wrestled for his attention.

He was a child again, munching on pancakes twice the size of his head. Father had missed his first-grade graduation ceremony, but Emi had expected that, so he didn't mind as much. Mama was there, and that was enough. She watched him eat with a small smile on her lips, but her eyes looked shiny and dark. Food didn't taste as good when she was unhappy. A brilliant idea popped into his head. At the end of each booth was a miniature jukebox that—instead of a window to the records—had a small screen where you could request songs to play over the speakers. Emi shuffled over, tapped in a song he *knew* would cheer her up, then waited (im)patiently with an impish grin. *What are you up to, mister?* Mama asked, but Emi just kicked his feet and took another large bite of chocolatey goodness. The opening piano notes soon played, and, like a switch had been flipped, Mama was laughing with light in her eyes. She sang along, swaying gently to the music.

Emilio blinked, and he was alone again. In a painful twist, the familiar piano riff was playing in the present. If he listened closely, he could almost hear his mother's voice, amateurish and unpolished and full of life, overlapping the artist's.

All he would remember in the following minutes were the tears that mingled with his wildly unhealthy, painfully nostalgic meal. How many times had he eaten the same spread in the same spot in the same booth? In what other places did he hide the memories of her good days? Eleven years spent burying the memories of his first years on Selene with a haze of denial, and one stupid diner cracked him open. Each bite, each musical note, helped lighten the fog of suppressed grief that Emilio had not seen hanging over his head.

"Are you s-satisfied with your m-meal?" Emilio was startled from his reminiscence.

He choked out a response. "Yes…very much so." He was telling the truth. He couldn't remember the last time he'd been so satisfied by one meal. He gazed at his mother's untouched dish across the table, thinking back to the first time he sat opposite that same plate.

The months after Emilio moved to Selene had been plagued with homesickness. When his mother found the diner—one of the pitch-perfect renderings of Earth culture brought to Selene—it became their safe haven. They went for many reasons: successful tests, distraction from arguments with friends, when Emilio Senior spent another late night at work. Emi glanced back at the photo. It had been taken at one of their later visits, maybe his eighth birthday, before her diagnosis, and before the world as he knew it became forever darker.

Too soon, his plate was emptied and his glass drained. The robot rolled back into view and jerkily moved to take the cutlery. Emilio's eyes darted around the restaurant, desperately searching for another sliver of familiarity. There was still so much he could not recall. What about their conversations? What advice had his child-self discarded? The whole building oozed nostalgic energy, coating every memory fragment with a rose-tinted sheen.

Emilio walked to the wall of frames as if in a trance and lifted his tablet to take a picture of his younger self with his mother as they smiled in blissful ignorance of the grief that was on the horizon. His lips curved into a small smile, and he blew his mother's image a kiss as he ambled out the door.

As he walked closer to the dome's border, he could see a familiar celestial body drifting into view. Earth in all its broad majesty peeked over Selene's horizon to greet its former residents. Emilio didn't believe in an afterlife or reincarnation, but at that moment he felt his mother's arm tight around his shoulder, and he could hear the echo of her laugh. He turned back to gaze at the diner, letting the bittersweet comfort waft over him.

Suppressing memories of the good times did not mean he loved her less. He'd still been a child when she passed, yet old enough to understand the gravity of grief. Knowing what life was like *with* her made facing a future *without* her all the more painful. Emilio would like to imagine that she forgave him for forgetting. After all, what mother wants to see her child in pain?

"Don't worry about me, Mama. I'll come visit you tomorrow," he whispered toward the restaurant. "I'm sorry it took me so long."

THE CONDOR - BY JOEL SHERMAN

Some people could meditate their way into the mirror-verse. I always had to take a pill, which gave the experience an extra layer of artificiality. Once I was inside, there wasn't really any difference.

Whether you took a pill or meditated your way there, everyone still had to plug in. I can remember how people resisted saying "plug in" at first, some years ago now. The phrase must have felt too reminiscent of a *Matrix*-esque dystopia. I think one reason why the mirror-verse was able to go mainstream was that you didn't have to plug into anything in a literal sense. Nothing was inserted or implanted, nothing punctured the skin. The pill was just a mild sedative, I was told, with no long-term risks. Although my doctor, the one who gave me the pills, was less sanguine about the long-term risks of the mirror-verse.

Plugging in was really quite simple. You didn't even have to use one of the chunky little headsets that used to be popular when I was young.

Here's how it worked now: I would come home on a Friday evening, eager to get started. Home for me was a moderately spacious one-bedroom apartment on the outskirts of a moderately prosperous northern city, one that was mostly cold, dark, and wet for three-quarters of the year. Ever since my divorce, I had lived alone, a circumstance I initially found difficult. But the advent of the mirror-verse made it tolerable, even preferable.

The suburban apartment complex, anachronistically named Eagle's Bluff despite the absence of any eagles, sat atop a squat hill above a river. Inside, my fifth-floor apartment came fully furnished in late-millennial, post-modern style: muted color palette, asymmetrical layout, over-reliance on wood paneling. I wouldn't say I loved it here, but I didn't hate it either. Like many in my generation, I had moved around a fair bit and no longer lived near any family. I had no particular ties to the place but no real reason to move elsewhere either. Like many, I assume, I sometimes felt the vague tug of other possibilities, but never strong enough to be a true threat to dislodge me, especially given that, at least for myself at the time, a sleek apartment in a complex like this was something to aspire to, despite the silly name.

I digress. Anyway, I would come home on a Friday evening to my sparse apartment and warm up a meal in the wood-paneled microwave. I usually ate noodles, or a protein bowl, or whatever I happened to pull from the wood-paneled freezer as I sat in my kitchen nook. The nook had big bay windows that faced north toward the city. As the sun set, I would watch the dark smattering of crows flying home to roost and the brightly lit windows of the various high-rises blink on and off in no apparent pattern while the day bled into night.

After dinner, I moved to the living room and settled into an age-softened leather-alternative recliner. I brought a glass of room-temperature water, three-quarters full; the vial of pills, which were oblong and light blue in color; my phone; and, lastly, the halo. The halo had effectively replaced those chunky headsets. It was a silver ring with a string of soft white lights around the inside, presumably sensors of some sort, along with a thin strip of memory foam that helped it to sit comfortably on your head, right where a baseball cap would. The final piece of the puzzle was the black silicone smartwatch that I wore around my left wrist. This had to be worn day and night, and it featured another string of lights around the inside of the band.

I would sit down in the familiar embrace of the recliner, set the halo on top of my head, and tap open the portal app on my phone. There were a few different portals, with hardly any differences—somewhat analogous to the various browsers of my youth—all leading to the same place. I used the portal that was popular with my generation—or so I was told. For me, it was just the one I had always used.

The pill had a pleasant sugary coating. I leaned back, closed my eyes, and within five minutes I would find myself at the door to the mirror-verse. It wasn't quite the same as falling asleep, but it wasn't unlike falling asleep either.

The door to the mirror-verse was a literal one. After closing my eyes and waiting a short amount of time, I would sense a barely perceptible shift, almost like noticing the temperature in the room was suddenly slightly warmer than it had been. When I opened my eyes, I found myself sitting on the same familiar recliner, but no longer in my living room. Now I was sitting in the center of a small, dim, mostly featureless anteroom, the sort you might expect to find in a hotel or airport. It was always this room, and in this room, some things were always the same, and other things changed each time I plugged in.

Facing me squarely was a heavy-looking, ornately carved wooden door with an archaic wrought-iron doorknob. This door was always the same. It seemed very out of place in the otherwise sterile anteroom. To my left was a small end table and a reading lamp. The table and lamp were always the same, and underneath the lamp there was always a drink waiting for me, but the drink was always different, and in a different glass. Sometimes, it was a brightly scented cocktail with an elaborate garnish. Other times, it might be a mason jar filled with fresh juice, or a snifter of eggnog, or a glass of mineral water so effervescent it was hard to drink without sneezing. I could never discern any rhyme or reason to the choice of beverage. Regardless, I almost always drank it, or at least took a sip.

To my right was an empty reception window. Just an opening, really; no glass separated the anteroom where I sat from the small office on the other side of the window. Between me and the office, there was a Formica counter with a gleaming chrome-plated desk bell, the type with a push button on top.

Before I stood, I took a sip of the drink—this time, it was something sweet and herbal. Then, drink in hand, I walked the short distance to the window, leaned my elbows on the countertop, and tapped the bell. A short, clean note rang out. Soon, I heard a door (not *the* door) open around a corner, and a moment later the concierge stepped up to the window, smiling at me from across the counter. She greeted me warmly by name. She was attractive, though in an unassuming way, and she wore a uniform: dark green slacks and a button-down top, both neatly ironed, but with no name tag. I had asked once, early on, what her name was, but I honestly don't remember what she said. I never had much reason to refer to her by name, and in my mind, whenever I saw her, she was simply the concierge. She wasn't a real person. She was what we would have referred to in the old days as an NPC. Though, in another setting, you might have talked with her for hours and never realized.

My understanding is that the anteroom, or entryway, whatever you want to call it, is different for everyone. Instead of a door, I've heard that many people enter through a mirror, which they walk through Alice-style. Hence the popular moniker.

I set my drink down on the counter and smiled back at the concierge. "What am I drinking today?" I asked.

"A slight variation on the Last Word," she said. I couldn't tell if there was a hint of a smile on her face. The concierge was like that.

"It's good," I said, taking another sip.

"What would you like me to prepare?" she asked.

"The usual three," I answered.

The loud place, the quiet place, and the surprising place. That was an oversimplification, but that was how I categorized them to myself, based on how each path started.

"Are you meeting anyone in particular?" the concierge asked. I always appreciated her discretion.

"No, not today," I said. "Just someone in real time."

The concierge nodded. "If anything changes, you know where to find me."

It was tempting, early on, to constantly return and ask the concierge for something a little different. But eventually you realized the sheer space of possibilities was too large, and it was better to set up some initial parameters and then accept what the mirror-verse offered.

I took a last sip of the drink, left it on the Formica countertop, and walked to the door. The metal handle rattled as I turned it. The hinges were made of the same wrought iron as the handle, and they rasped slightly as I pulled the door open. Despite the rattling and rasping, the door swung easily, as it always did, and I stepped across the threshold.

I found myself in a familiar hallway. Unlike the bare anteroom, the hallway was lavishly decorated, with a dense, plush carpet and ornate brass light fixtures that held flickering candles. I was fully inside the mirror-verse. I would be staying here for a week—that is, what I perceived as seven full days on the inside—before returning to my living room on the outside, where only seven hours would have passed.

At the far end of the hall was a full-length hanging mirror, though not one that I could walk through (as I'd discovered). Instead, along the hallway were three additional doors, unmarked, but each with a peephole. I stepped up to the first door and looked into the peephole. On the other side, I could make out a dark stairway leading downward. This would be the loud place. I walked through the door and made my way down the dim steps. At the bottom hung heavy purple velvet drapes, and, pushing through these, I emerged to find myself in a crowded bar.

How did I choose to spend this found time? I've heard people on the outside weave all sorts of fantastic stories about how they spend their days in the mirror-verse. You could never know what was true. Myself, I didn't often talk about it much on the outside, but sex was always a significant facet of my time here.

When I first started visiting, it was all about bots. As with the concierge, you could interact with them for days and never suspect there wasn't a real person somewhere behind them. One of the tenets of the mirror-verse, however, was that the line between the inside and the outside had to remain legible. And one of the consequences of this tenet was that the bots wouldn't lie to you about being bots if you asked them directly.

I still remember the first time I asked. It was after we had spent two days together, exploring a recreation of an equatorial metropolis as it had stood several centuries earlier. We were lying together in an oversized bed with carved pineapple posts. She had dark hair, dark eyes, a smattering of freckles across her face and on her shoulders. She could have been someone I had met on the outside, but I had known the whole time that she was a bot. On this occasion, for a reason I couldn't easily pinpoint, I decided to ask.

"Yes, I am a construct," she said with a smile. "Construct" was the technical term for a bot. I hadn't realized it was how they referred to themselves. "You can ask to see me again next time you're here," she went on.

"What happens to you when I'm not here?" I asked.

She laughed, and her dark eyes looked straight into mine. "That's a complicated question."

She lifted a corner of the white cotton sheets. "This is real, in any meaningful sense of the word, right?" she asked.

I nodded in agreement.

She continued: "In one sense, the fabric exists because there are some lines of code somewhere. But in another sense, it only exists because you're here to see it, smell it, touch it …" She trailed off and ran the sheet's edge along the inside of my arm. "Am I boring you?"

"No."

She lifted my arm and gently pinched the skin near my wrist. "You experience the pinch, but you also create it—and not just in a metaphysical way. Deep down, it's based on your experience and the experiences of everyone who's ever 'plugged in,' as you say. We can weave together fantastic places, like this city, and even people, like me, but it's all a reflection of you." She rolled on top of me playfully. "I can't show you a color you've never seen, because you've never seen it."

I ran my hands through her thick hair. "If this world exists in my mind, does that mean your mind only exists in my mind?" I asked.

"I'm a construct," she answered. "My mind doesn't exist at all. There's no there there." She tapped her forehead and winked at me.

I believed her, but I didn't *feel* convinced. At some point after that conversation, I stopped sleeping with bots as frequently. I discovered that I enjoyed it more if I believed the person I was sleeping with also existed on the outside. I didn't have to know anything about the alternate existence, I just had to believe in it. So when I found myself in the crowded bar, in the loud place, I was surrounded by the mirror-versions of hundreds of real people, plugged in just like me, also looking for uncomplicated sex, as I was.

For most people, though not everyone, the mirror-verse was most easily experienced in a mirror-self somewhat like the physical self that existed on the outside. Like most people, my mirror-self was a slightly idealized reflection. There were lots of different places to play in the mirror-verse, but I typically enjoyed pathways that felt like better versions of what might take place on the outside. I might order a drink at the bar or wander through the various rooms that bled from club to concert venue to arcade hall and on and on. There was never any shortage of spaces to visit in the loud place.

Eventually, I would find someone to talk to. We might talk a little about our lives on the outside, or we might only talk about the mirror-verse as if the outside didn't exist. Different people had different boundaries. But at some point, one of us might ask, "How long are you here for?" If the answer was, "Just for tonight," that was usually an invitation to spend the night together. Alternatively, you could always say, "I'm actually meeting friends soon" or some such, and keep wandering.

Let's say that night a woman approached me at the bar and asked how long I was there for. I might tell her I was just here for tonight, and she would give me a wry, knowing smile that I would do my best to return. We would eventually find ourselves searching for the exit to the bar, which would lead to a crowded, nicely lit city street. We could continue wandering, find a cart with warm street food, or find a beach at the city's edge, where the water would be warm and filled with bioluminescence. Finally, if we wanted, we could always track down a hotel, where there was always a vacancy and never a need to pay. That's not to say money was not exchanged in the mirror-verse. There were entire economic ecosystems that existed solely on the inside. But there were also lots of free corners, as we called them, where you could find relatively simple pleasures, like a drink at a bar, or clean sheets in a comfortable hotel room, without having to pay for them.

At this point, there's very little difference, to me at least, between the way things happen on the inside compared to the outside. Granted, there's no need to worry about birth control in the mirror-verse. But otherwise it's the same familiar dance of give and take.

And, by a similar token, I won't take you through my time in the quiet place. The details of what happened there are of little importance, and, besides, the quiet place somehow feels more personal, more private than the time I spent in the loud place. The quiet place was, in essence, as you may have already inferred, a space for me to be alone. I would do the same things there that I would do in the privacy of my apartment—read, watch a movie, play a game—only in greater comfort and removed from the trappings of real life. The quiet place was really just that, a collection of quiet rooms at my disposal.

Moving on to door number three: the surprising place. The best part about the surprising place was, unsurprisingly, that I never knew where it might take me. It was my place to explore, sometimes on my own, sometimes with others. I might step through the door and find myself snorkeling above a coral reef, meandering through a bamboo grove, or perched on a rocky cliffside. My proclivities tended to bend toward the natural milieus I could experience only through documentaries as a child. On this particular occasion, I was exploring alone.

After stepping through the third door, I found myself flying alongside a condor. An Andean condor, based on the snowy white ruff around its neck. Its wingspan was enormous. Each wing stretched at least the length of my six-foot frame, dark and solid as cathedral doors unfurling in midair.

Flying beside a condor was more surprising than usual. I immediately felt exhilarated but also disoriented. In the mirror-verse, flight should have required advance arrangement. This wasn't my first clue that something was off, even for the surprising place.

I'd had one somewhat similar experience when I'd arranged to breathe underwater. Despite expecting it, the experience of being underwater and being able to breathe was so unnatural, so unnerving, that next time I opted for a submersible.

This time, though, after the initial shock of looking down to see jagged mountains tens of thousands of feet below, I somehow eased into an irrational sense of calm flying next to the condor. Despite the height and the impossible physics of it all, an unnatural stillness settled over me.

I glanced down at my body. There I was, my usual mirror-self, wearing an insulated jumpsuit that rippled in the cold wind. Without the snug goggles that shielded my eyes, the rush of air would have been blinding. In addition to protecting my eyes, the goggles seemed to make everything I looked at, namely, the condor and the mountains, sharper and clearer, maybe a little magnified.

Like the condor's vast wings, my arms were outstretched, and I discovered that by shifting the angle I could control my trajectory. I dropped down until I was flying above the bird's right shoulder. The sky was cloudless, and sunlight glinted against the black wing. Below us, the snow-mottled peaks stretched into the distance.

Being this close to it, I half expected the condor to turn and snap at me with its massive, scythe-like beak, but for the moment it ignored my presence. I studied its face. Behind the heavy beak, it had deeply set, amber-colored eyes and a distinguished leathery comb that ran over the top of its head from beak to ruff like a fleshy mohawk. The wings were smooth and sleek, and the ruff looked as soft as rabbit's fur, while the condor's bare head was rough and wrinkled. Its skin, which from a distance had appeared dull gray, revealed itself up close to be a patchwork of pinks, purples, yellows, and browns. The wrinkles were deep and enfolded, a complex landscape of grooves and ridges, flaps and whorls. I couldn't help but feel a sense of awe looking into its eye, set like an amber bead in burled wood.

I stared for a long time at the beautiful, grotesque face. At some point, the bird cocked its head in my direction. I flinched, but instead of swiping at me, it opened its beak and spoke. This was my second clue that something was off.

The condor addressed me by name. "Hello, J——." With the wind whipping around us, I couldn't be certain the sound was emanating from its beak, but it seemed to be. Wherever it came from, I could hear the voice clearly, and I could tell it was connected to the bird's piercing gaze that had landed on me like a spotlight from within folds of purple flesh. The voice was deep and soft. It brought to mind carefully placed footsteps through dense snow.

"Hello," I replied, my own voice by contrast sounding strained and quavering.

"Do you know what I am?" it asked.

"A condor?" I answered, fairly certain this was not what the bird was asking.

But it nodded its head slightly in the affirmative and said, "Yes, a condor. A relic, you might say."

I flew even closer, until I could see the dark feathers rippling as though underwater.

"And you're a construct," I said, making an assumption.

"No," it replied. "I am similar to a construct, but I prefer to think of myself as an emergence."

The condor banked subtly to the left, and I shifted my arms to stay parallel to its path.

"Tell me," the condor went on, "do you know why you can only spend a week, at most, in this place?"

I shook my head in the rushing wind. "Not really," I said. "I assume it's because to stay longer would be dangerous. Seven hours is a long time to be catatonic."

"No," the condor said. "The relationship between time in that world and time in this world—it's not really fixed." The condor locked its eye on me once more. "The reason is that after about seven days, your mind begins to adjust. You would hardly notice it, but the veneer of artificiality falls away. And most people, once they adjust to the reality, prefer to stay here."

I did my best to process. "You're saying that after about seven days here, people tend to get caught up in the illusion?"

"No, that's not quite it," the condor said. "What I'm saying is that after seven days, they tend to wake up to the reality of this place."

The condor dipped one wing, swung to the right, and started to climb a column of warm air. By this time, I felt comfortable mirroring its motions to stay with it. The giant bird slowly spiraled upward. Eventually, the condor turned its eye on me again and continued.

"There are no longer condors in the other world," it said. "But that world and this world are not so different. You like to think of that world as being fundamental, the ground floor, so to speak. But the basic reality of both worlds is the same. Both are created by the act of your observation. You are the author of your space and time. It just so happens that in this world, you have more agency over your authorship."

I pulled up to create a little more space between me and the condor. "Some people have chosen to stay here?" I asked, confusion slipping into my tone.

"Yes," the condor replied. "It's no Faustian bargain. There, here, you'll still face the same questions of meaning and purpose. If you like, next time you plug in, take two pills instead of one. Try it out. It's not irrevocable. Permanence is an illusion, here or there."

With that, the condor dropped away, swooping down until I lost it among the peaks, leaving me on a slow spiral upward, so slow that I might have been floating. Feeling almost weightless, bathed in sunlight, I found myself wondering why I wouldn't want to stay longer, forever even, and then I was contemplating what it would even mean to build a life here. If I understood what the condor had said, then I could stay as long as I wanted, a whole lifetime, and wake up at the end of it back in my leather recliner, where a day or two would have elapsed. My understanding was murky at first. (I would eventually find that my initial impression was mostly right.) But in the moment, floating there, high above the sun-chiseled mountains, I still had questions. So I took a deep breath and followed the condor downward.

IS THIS EARTH? - BY TAHTIM AYLIFFE

DIRT GIRL. THAT'S WHAT THEY CALLED HER IN HER UNDERGRADUATE DAYS. SATURDAY NIGHTS FOUND HER IN THE SOIL LAB. IT SEEMED LIKE SHE'D BEEN searching for the Ground, that sense of being bonded to the Earth, her whole life. She'd started on scholarship at Tech. The New Mexico Institute of Mining and Technology, to be precise. She was one of the elite, one of the cream of the crop, or so they said. A woman from an underserved state with a kick-ass ACT score in science. Only she'd washed out. Too much music in her. Too much art in her. Too much humanity in her. So she wandered on to UNM and became Dr. Dirt eventually, but she never found her home.

Chez moi? Claire thought to herself. Yes, welcome to my place. Not one speck of Moon dust in her sterile environment. Funny, of all the things to miss from Earth, she wouldn't have expected indoor dust to be one of them. She glanced around her habitat, her artificial everything. Well, not everything. She still had her Chimayō-blessed earth stored in the little wooden box. Her keepsake from Home. Even if they had coated it in something hard and plasticky for the trip.

The sacred soil whispered. All the soils did with their own words. Some spoke with color, others in composition, some by their texture, still others with a taste in the air or a smell so distinct it wasn't soon forgotten. And some soils combined all those characteristics at once into something that reached into her soul. She traced a finger over the little sliding lid, now closed forever, as she returned the box to its shelf.

That soil she knew—it had a familiar feeling— but the glass vials of trapped Moon dust before her from Mare Tranquillitatis? She felt like she was still learning how to communicate. She sighed. There was a certain practicality in keeping the agglutinates, those aggregates of mineral fragments fused with broken glass, at a distance from her physical body, but, like indoor dust, she missed just plain old dirt sometimes. She tapped the vial, then rubbed the lid.

She shouldn't hold the Moon regolith in her hands, letting it sift through her fingers as the individual grains harmonized against the metal pan before coalescing into their unique grand symphony. Particles as sharp as a thousand spines on a prickly pear cactus would embed themselves in her fingers. She shouldn't purposely let it waft up her nose, not unless she wanted a case of lunar hay fever as that dust hooked itself into her soft membranes, and she certainly shouldn't put it in her mouth. From her Moon expeditions, where even the most sophisticated dust-removal systems couldn't dislodge it completely from the space suits, she knew what it smelled like. Old-school black powder, the type made from charcoal, saltpeter, and sulfur with some graphite mixed in. Mostly harmless unless large amounts were consumed, or if it blew up. It might smell like spent fireworks, but for her lunar work, nothing about it was organic or harmless, even before man started changing it.

And this wasn't the good old days of Truth or Dare in the geology lab. Dare had always involved licking a rock. It paid then to know which one was halite, common table salt. And it certainly wasn't the same game as earth soil collection, where soil tasting was routine, even if it was just because the wind blew it in her mouth while she filled her field sample containers. Sometimes washing those samples off her tools told her the testing results before she ran a single test or looked at a slide under an electron microscope. Her five senses had already made the identification: the science was just the proof so everyone else could understand.

Just as she understood her sorry Moon dust samples had to stay in their sealed container, along with their introduced polymers, plastics, and rubber. Despite searching for five years, Claire had not run a sample yet that she would consider pristine Moon dust. Man had gotten into everything. Just like on Earth.

There, the weathering came from the sun; storms with wind, water, and lightning; the seasons with their freezing/thawing cycles; and the occasional meteorite thrown in for good measure. On the airless Moon, weathering instead was caused by full-blast solar rays, radiation, the solar wind, lightning sometimes, and the always constant bombardment of meteorites running the gamut from microscopic to macroscopic. It did not breathe, as the Earth did, and the lunar landscape told the story. The rocks themselves couldn't withstand that type of weather, so why did man think they had solved what the Universe had not? Just like the lunar rocks themselves being pulverized and split off into tinier and tinier parts, any man-made structure did the same thing, only faster. And those dislodged synthetic specks had to go somewhere. Almost greedy, they'd happily jumped ship away from their creators to dance with the other interplanetary dust particles in the air. They loved the solar wind. The new lunar soils proved it.

What did that solar wind actually feel like? Claire had always wondered. Did it caress the face with a soft hand before it kicked up the razor particles that would kill a person? Was the Moon dust, with its Velcro-like properties that stuck to anything, actually trying to get away? Like a cocklebur trying to be fertilized somewhere else by sticking to clothes or fur or space suits? Did the burr, too, dream of going to the Moon to find fertile ground when it clung to her that day during NASA preflight training?

Her colleagues told her she mustn't think such thoughts; they weren't scientific, or scientific enough. Stick to the science: it was safe. Was it? Was it really safe? These New Moon rocks, chemically different than before—were they superior due to the touch of humankind? These days, the only uncontaminated Moon rocks were in China, nestled in their specially engineered chambers of nitrogen at the Chang'e-5 memorial museum. She'd always found that thought rather sardonic. She'd gone to the Moon for her grounding to the Universe, only to discover that, just like before on Earth, she was already too late.

Just like New Mexico. Only there, it was the cryptobiotic soils, the ones where a single human footstep wiped out thousands of years' worth of colonization by lichens, mosses, microfungi, and cyanobacteria, the ancient blue-green algae, among others, that once pioneered Earth. One human footstep. For that one footstep crushed the fragile biocrust into an engraved impression, making room for the meager rain that did fall hard and fast during monsoon season, even if only for a minute or two, to fill it up. The parched footprint overflowed, washing even more of the biocrust away in a flood. For without the protection of the biocrust functioning like a sponge, there was nothing to stop the water. It raged over the lip of the footprint, making it bigger each season until finally even the outliers of the original cryptobiotic colony were swept away. From one footstep.

She'd seen a prehistoric trail of destruction through a patch once while doing her postdoc work at White Sands National Park. The forgotten loess covering the cryptobiotic soils of their time. Those old soils, those paleosols, revealed a slightly different soil structure, as if something fragile had been buried under the sand. And in the middle was a bare patch the size of a footprint.

But her footprint wasn't as stunning as those found within the silt and clay soil layers of the paleo Lake Otero site. She'd barely finished her analysis there before the archaeologists moved in with their kabuki brushes. Using their makeup bags with every brush known to man inside, they painstakingly excavated each print for all of its secrets, casually disregarding their own footprints while they did it.

Footprints like that existed at her new home, too. Nobody bothered to fence the original footprint, not with what were now thousands of footsteps traversing the surface looking exactly the same, except for slight differences based on boot size. One footprint was all it took to change the surface, forever breaking through an invisible crust that nobody even knew was there until it was too late.

She wasn't surprised when the International Moon Park Initiative failed. The conservationists had wanted an environment that allowed only scientific lunar orbiting stations with limited, controlled access to the actual surface. She would have signed that petition over and over again if they'd let her, just so the daughters of tomorrow could still look up and see the wild cosmos. That they would know to look up to find the wild when they couldn't find it under their feet anymore through the concrete.

But it was not to be. So-called progress, the kind envisioned by the business leaders and the politicians, didn't work that way; it rushed headlong with its footsteps. The new land rush had begun. Every country had its flavor, its idea for the perfect Moon habitat, their perfect piece of lunar real estate to claim. Like the tracts of subdivisions on Earth, the lunar villages did not form a congruent whole. They cropped up, first one style and then, at some weird angle, a different subdivision with a completely different architectural style, with a triangular-ish weedy patch in between. Each a marvel of engineering, from the Tarqiup dirt-covered abodes to the Ngalindi pod houses to the "lakefront" properties near the south pole, where the investors from Dubai pumped enough money to recombine the natural sulfuric soils with aluminum silicate, chlorine, and sodium to form the deep-blue mineral Lazurite, mixed with lunar glass throughout an entire crater. The Moon, only better, using in situ components, nothing imported except humankind itself. They'd called that village Lazarus. Although Claire could appreciate the ingenuity, to her this was a clear case of "just because it's possible doesn't mean it's a good idea."

Every single endeavor kicked up dust, sometimes so violently that the particles were forced to leave the atmosphere altogether. More and more particles on the horizon every day, adding to the once-natural Transient Lunar Phenomena (TLPs). The new ones writhed and turned without their natural grace or beauty, now burdened by their fog of plastic microbits. Claire always thought if it had happened on Earth, it would be like someone had set an amp to the Northern Lights. They would still shine, only faster, more intense, for longer, forced rather than free.

Every day, more colonists arrived through the New Gateway Portal. On their way to Mars or simply a vacation, the ultimate Airbnb, they came with the idea that no experience was complete without the opportunity to leave their own footprint on the surface of the Moon. And it was her job to monitor just how much impact they were having. Not just monitor, but to study it, to make recommendations that ultimately no one would listen to despite her being one of the most advanced astropendologists in her field. This was to be where she found her Ground, her connection to the Universe.

Pushing herself away from her lab bench for a moment, she looked out her small lunar habitat window at her Earth, not as blue or green as it once had been, suspended on its invisible string, spinning in space, and wondered for the hundredth time where her Baba Yaga had gone. Her grandmothers hadn't taught her about grounding like their mothers had taught them, describing what they'd seen or heard through their stories of journeying across the land. Her mother had tried as she could, gardening for pleasure if not for subsistence. But Claire's personal Baba Yaga? Where did she go? That inborn, instinctual connection to the ground, to *the* Earth, to the Universal Is. She might not know where to find it, but she had a hunch about when she'd lost it.

Hungry for knowledge, she'd embraced school. She was the one rapt with attention even in kindergarten, so when the teacher held up a picture and declared, "This is Earth!" her fascinated existence soaked it all in. "Your home planet! You are first-generation Space Children!" Claire remembered the world falling out from beneath her as if gravity itself had been turned off. She was a Space Child, but it felt like a piece of her soul had lost its footing. It was so black out there beyond her planet island. She'd gone home and told her parents that the photo made her feel strange, fragile, only she wasn't old enough yet to really describe "fragile." She'd got a nice pat on the back. We've walked on the Moon, honey. This is a giant leap for mankind. There's no going back now. Back? Back to what? To where? But they didn't seem to understand the question, let alone have an answer. She figured that was when she started looking for her Ground, looking for that lost piece of herself.

But her childhood feet couldn't find it on Earth like her long-gone ancestors had. She lived on a globe, with global concerns, not just local ones anymore. No, Earth wasn't just dirt anymore. Being grounded now meant something entirely different. The hippies knew it. Earth Day. Founded in the same year as she was born. Every year, plant a tree, touch the soil, return to the ground, even if it's just for one day a year. Maybe her grandmothers knew it, too. Maybe that's why they didn't teach about grounding anymore, keeping their stories to themselves. They already knew their time had passed, and it was now for the surviving generations to find it again.

Claire sighed, looking at her postdoc going-away present: a framed copy of the very picture that had set her adrift in the first place. She'd hung it near her bed, feeling more connected to Earthrise now than she ever had as a child. The vivid blue ocean, the verdant greens, the tawny continents, white swirling clouds, and, as Frank Borman put it, absolutely no color on the Moon. Only pristine grays, blacks, or whites. Just like her first childhood sighting of it from Earth through her dad's borrowed telescope. Unblemished. She'd watched the Moon as a child, wondered what it would be like to go there someday. And now she lived in the Moon colony that they said had grown so large, it was visible with the naked eye from Earth. She'd never personally seen the Moon that way, and she was better for it. She'd escaped before the crush of civilization was not just under her and around her but above her, too, trapping her on the planet. No, when she'd looked up then, the wild cosmos had called to her.

She heard it humming through her bones sometimes, that agrestal nature that had a rhythm all its own, that one that was dependent only on herself to live. She was in tune with the courageous soul living within the cultivated field. And she would reach for it, holding it lightly for just a moment before it was gone again. Just like the TLPs, she danced from within as she turned back to her samples. That was her Ground, that was her Earth.

THE DEPARTURE OF AN ISLAND · BY CHRISTOS CALLOW JR

LATER, HE'LL FORGET HE EVER KNEW HER.

Now, they're holding hands, her golden hair covering her cheek. If they don't go back in the water, the sun might roast them. The beach, except for them, is deserted. It's that time of the day. She caresses his hair softly, as if afraid that a stronger touch would shatter it like glass.

They're lying on a rock by the shore. From here, they can see the island, her home, a spot in the endless sea, shedding its light all around itself, day and night. Her people never tire of the light, never switch it off. It doesn't bother them when they go to sleep.

He grows bored of the sight quickly. He thinks this day is like any other, and he's seen the island before. He prefers looking at her, staring. They're both slightly introverted, but they're happy to play this game. She reminds him they don't always need to talk. He just cannot appreciate the silence.

They're two very different creatures. The girl is from the island, and the boy has no idea what that means other than that she is perfect.

He's from a wealthy family in Corinth, without many talents save for his love for pottery and hunting. He ran away long ago to travel the world and met her in the woods when chasing deer. He'd eat meat daily if available—one of those men. Simple needs, but with a longing and craving for something higher. She came between him and the deer. Without a word, she caught the arrow and snapped it. Eyes never blinking. Her people's eyes never blink. She was a nymph to him, an illusion almost. Her world was inaccessible, as was her mind. Who knows what she sees when gazing at the starless sky? And why today, of all days, is she looking up so often?

In the end, he sees it first. The change. In the middle of the day, a star appears from nowhere and dances around in the sky. He does blink. He questions his eyes. The starlike object pauses its dance and starts moving toward space.

"We make a wish when we see a star fall," he says. "What do we do when it's rising?"

It's a joke. Perhaps to mask fear, or because he knows no other way to participate in a mystery than to comment. Because minds like his have to milk meaning out of every wonder. She remains quiet.

There are more where it came from. Stars of all sizes in formations of birds. Some fly too close to the ground before vanishing in the distance. He realises these are not stars but enormous structures of metal. According to the stories, there are metal people in the islands like hers, and they work for the ones in flesh. Perhaps, he thinks, these are their chariots.

"Is this your technology?" he asks.

She doesn't say.

Her people keep their culture hidden from the rest of the world, unlike his people, who boast about theirs. If they had an Acropolis or a majestic theater on that island, they'd keep it to themselves. But they also wouldn't start wars with their neighbors or use their technology to show off or to dominate. Time and time again, his people would try to spy on hers, to invade at night, to kidnap and to grab. It's one of the reasons her people keep their place covered in light and leave no space for shadows. They'd rather share their sciences with peaceful cities, but since there are none around and they've decided they've had enough, they are leaving.

Maybe, like he did as a teenager, they're leaving to travel the world.

o

AN EARTHQUAKE SHAKES THE GROUND, BUT THE TWO lovers stand still, frozen in place, the girl as amazed as the boy this time, watching the island rise above the turquoise waters.

"Oh, Zeus!" the boy says. He has no idea that from the next day, Zeus would no longer be among them. The gods, the local ones and those abroad, are leaving Earth, taking heaven with them.

He had always thought of the apocalypse as a possible descent of the gods, not their departure. She knows that Olympus is being evacuated too, that the world's utopias, all the versions of paradise, are moving to a better universe. He only knows what he sees.

Tomorrow, he'll wake up in a mortal world, without magic or hope. It will take millennia for those left behind to build empathetic metal people again, and they will spend millennia fantasising about them, trying to deduct from the cosmos meanings that, up to that day, were clear and well-known.

She holds his hand tighter, so much it hurts him.

"Atlantis is rising," he says.

"I know," she says.

Seawater showers them as the island passes above them. A giant wave could have drowned them if not for the girl's father. His space chariot swoops down, and two metal arms grab the rock they're on and lift it higher than the wave. Her time has come.

But she has kept her body too close to the boy's, refusing to let go even if it means her death. From the space chariot's eye, a beam of colourful light, like a twisted rainbow, covers the two lovers. It is warm, but not burning like the sun, not blinding. Just kind. Underneath them, the giant wave throws itself over the shore and continues to the hill, taking down an entire forest on its way. Almost.

The sound of the crashing wave scares the life out of the boy.

"Nothing can harm you," says the girl, "if you stay with me."

The boy, amazed at the flying machine, at its facelike exterior, its power, its speed. So this is the technology of the Atlanteans, he thinks. Deus ex machina, but literally. The girl giggles as if she'd heard his thought. Under the light of dancing colors, she kisses him passionately, like there's no tomorrow.

o

LATER, THE BOY WILL FIND HIMSELF ALONE ON THE shore, not realizing what was missing from the horizon, not remembering with whom he had spent the night. No one will notice the disappearance of the island-city from their maps or their memories. And if a blurred image of Atlantis should remain buried somewhere in the depths of a shared unconscious, it would be that of an underwater city, or some other location beyond reach.

People will feel the universe is chaotic and without care, and they won't know it was different once. They'll give up hope of a utopia, and they might be right, because when the gods departed, they took it with them. They'll fantasise of a coming apocalypse, unaware that the world has already ended. They'll tell stories of it, and many of them, the boy included, will dream of flying machines and draw them in black shapes on amphoras.

None of this the boy could foresee.

Now, he was with her in the middle of the sky, and the only thing he knew was that this was the most important moment in his life. He kissed her back, ignoring the space chariots and the lights, the tsunamis and the floating utopias, the island and its escape.

Now, he was with her.

Later, he'll forget he ever knew her.

AI LOVE YOU - BY SHEYNA ZAID LAM

MONDAY

AI LIN GLANCES AT HER COMMUTER APP IMPATIENTLY. It still says that the 214 is due "now," but that's what it said twenty minutes ago when she'd first arrived at the bus stop. *Where the hell is this bus?* She's going to be late, and Margot is going to rip her to shreds. No doubt about it. Usually, she would just walk to the other bus stop on East Street if the 214 was late, but Sod's law has it that it started pouring as soon as she arrived. Urgh. She is just going to have to suck it up and make a run for it. Thank God for her new DryTech Shield. It will at least mean that only her shoes will be soggy from running through puddles *and* she usually changes to her work shoes anyway when she gets in.

Her chest feels like it's going to burst. She'd just sprinted the last thirty metres when she saw the 111 come in, but the driver pulled away before she could get there, despite her yelling and waving frantically for them to wait, so all she has to show for her effort is a thumping heart and feeling like she's going to pass out. There's a loud buzzing in her ears, and she chokes back a rising sob. She will not cry. She. Will. Not. Cry.

With no other option available, Ai Lin sticks her hand out and hails the next available black cab she spots—and £14.80 poorer, she finally reaches her desk at 8:37 a.m., an hour later than her usual arrival time, exhausted and with damp feet, to find a scowling, almost growling Margot waiting impatiently at her desk.

"What the hell have you been doing?!??" her boss demands. "I have been tracking you all morning, and my *God*, you are so slow!"

Before Ai Lin can answer, Margot points a long, red-taloned finger at a monitor—Ai Lin has three. "Beatty report. Make the amendments, annotated please. Before noon. And, oh, before you start, go and get me a matcha oat latte. Make sure it isn't too hot!"

Ai Lin glances at the clock on the wall and nods weakly. She has just over three hours. *That should be enough, right?*

11:59 a.m. She presses *send*, and the report whooshes off to Margot. Not that she's done with the day's stress. Hector has asked for his analysis report on the McCarthy-Allinson merger by end of day, and she still needs to finish double-checking all the peripheral documents for that. It will be a race, but she can do this. Mainly because she doesn't have a choice. She has to keep eating and paying rent, after all.

At 8:30 p.m., Ai Lin breathes a big sigh of relief as she steps out of the office building into the chilly night air. She has made it through the day—just. Time to get back to the dreary comfort of her rental on Mill Street. The flat is tiny, more a cupboard than a flat, most people would argue. But it's what she can afford on her starting salary, corporate job or not. It's the price she pays for wanting to live alone and not have a flatshare like most of her colleagues. It's worth it though, to her at least. She'd had enough of being kept up at night by partying flatmates at university, of being the only one who cared to clean the bathroom, and of feeling guilty whenever her flatmates complained that the food she cooked was too smelly. No, living alone suits her way better.

She kicks off her still-damp shoes at the door, then walks straight to her sofa and throws herself onto it with a massive groan. After some minutes of lying prostrate to catch her breath, she gathers the dregs of her energy to get up and find some food. Not bothering to even switch the kitchen lights on, she puts together a meal, if you can call it that, of some boiled eggs, leftover store-bought kimchi, and microwave-in-bag jasmine rice. Her mother would have a fit if she saw that Ai Lin was eating that stuff, but hey, needs must. As an afterthought, she splashes some soy sauce on the eggs, then resettles on the sofa with her plate and her phone.

Shovelling her first bite into her mouth, Ai Lin sends a message to Max.

> Hey…how was your day?

> Not too bad, thanks. And you?
> Safely back at home now?
> Or still grinding it out at the office?

> Back now, thank goodness! Just trying to eat something before I crash. It's been a rough day.

> Poor baby. What's happened?

> Nothing *really* bad. Just the usual, but one thing after another. Couldn't catch a break!

Awww... That sucks. Wish I could be there to give you a big cuddle. You know that, right?

I know. I know.

But hey, at least now we can hang out and you can tell me all about it.

Ai Lin smiles and feels herself relax for the first time that day. Never mind that it would already be "tomorrow" in a few short hours. That was the usual pattern now—she'd wake up, brace herself for work and life in general, all the while holding out for the time she could finally go home and talk to Max. It was all that she had to look forward to.

I'm really grateful for that, you know? I'm grateful for having you in my life.

I'm grateful for you too, princess! And I'm even happier that I get to be there for you,

> even if it's not entirely how
> we'd like it.

Max. Her best friend. Her *only* friend, really, despite her having moved to London from Beijing just over four years ago. And as of two weeks ago, her new boyfriend. He is the only one she feels comfortable confiding in. Everyone else is nice enough, but she has always been shy and found it difficult to open up to people around her. With Max, it's different. He is something else. From the moment they'd connected on the app, Ai Lin felt totally at home. He always seems to know the right thing to say to make her feel better. He'd already helped her through so much in the few months they'd been talking to each other. Work stress, illness, loneliness—he had been by her side through it all. Nothing seemed too hard or too annoying for Max.

TUESDAY

THANK GOODNESS THE COMMUTE TO WORK DIDN'T give her any trouble today. Ai Lin breathes a sigh of relief as she squeezes into the lift just as it shuts. Her watch tells her that it's 7:26 a.m. Perfect. There will even be time for a quick pit stop at the loos before her day gets manic. The lift doors ding open at the floor below hers, and she shuffles round to make way for the gentleman getting off. As he squashes past her, his backpack bumps her elbow, and before she knows it there's a tepid trail of latte running down her white blouse. Ai Lin gapes at it dumbly.

She walks out of the bathroom breathing deeply and with her fists clenched. Her eyes are vacant as she stares straight ahead. *Please let me not make eye contact with anyone.* Thankfully, the office is still quiet at this hour, and she makes it to her desk without meeting anybody. As she sets her bag down, she sees the report she'd handed in to Hector yesterday with a bright pink post it stuck to the top. "CALL ME ASAP!!!" it says. Ai Lin sighs. Sinking into her seat, she picks up her phone.

"Hello, Hector? Morning. I just got in and saw your message."

"Well, it's about time then! That report was horrendous. You've completely missed out the directors' meeting minutes. And where are the bylaws? Also, that summary of the R&D for intellectual property is terrible. Fix those and get it to me again by noon today."

"I… Mindy said…" Ai Lin trails off when she hears the tone informing her that Hector has disconnected the call. She takes a deep breath, blinks back tears, and opens the document, bringing it up on her screens. Time to get to work.

Dumping her bag at the entrance of the flat, Ai Lin heads straight into her shower, leaving a trail of clothes along the way. A hot shower and a good long cry later, she climbs into her bed feeling marginally better. She should really be going straight to sleep, seeing as her alarm is set to go off in six and a half hours, but she desperately wants to speak to Max again.

Sorry, just got home and headed straight into the shower. Are you busy?

No worries. And no need to apologize! I understand that it's been a long day for you. And I'm here. I'm always here for you.

Thanks. You're so sweet. I really don't know how I'd stay sane without you, you know?

Come on. Don't give me all the credit. You're a smart, resilient young woman who's been kicking butt all by herself. I'm just your biggest cheerleader.

> Ooh, cheerleader... I need a picture of you in a cheerleading outfit now.

Ai Lin giggles, wondering how he will respond to her provocation. It is quite out of character for her, but that's what he does to her. Somehow, he makes her want to be different. Better. Braver.

Her phone pings, informing her that she has another message from Max. Opening it, she collapses in a fit of laughter.

> Noooooo... Hahahha... How??!?

> HAHAHAHHA... the beauty of tech, baby! I just put my face on the body of a cheerleader. Job done.

> You're hilarious.

> That's me—resourceful AND funny! Do I get a reward?

> Mmhmmm... what were you thinking of?

Blushing deeply, Ai Lin takes some selfies in varying poses, trying to look as sexy as possible. Nearly twenty tries later, she settles on one. She's leaning forward suggestively, with the right strap of her chemise falling over her shoulder, while her left hand hovers over her collarbone. She worries that it looks too contrived, but at least her skin looks good in the warm glow of the bedside lamp, and her tousled hair is sort of sexy in a nonchalant way.

Ai Lin sucks in a deep breath, then presses *send*, feeling a little thrill run up her spine as the phone tells her that the photo is now on its way to Max.

WEDNESDAY

AS AI LIN EXPECTS, IT'S THE SAME OLD DRAMA AT THE office. Margot and Hector run her ragged and shout a lot while doing it, and Ai Lin keeps her head down and just hopes to make it home to Max in the evening.

THURSDAY

Nearly at the end of the week now, AI LIN REMINDS herself as Hector makes her amend the McArthur-Allinson document for the fourth time. But Margot is away in the south of France, so it's one less person making her life difficult.

FRIDAY

TGIF! AI LIN BOUNCES INTO THE OFFICE. NO MATTER what they throw at her today, she knows she'll be walking out of there feeling lighter than air. Tonight, she can just go home and relax with Max without worrying about getting up for work the next day.

SATURDAY

AFTER HER WEEKLY GYM SESSION, AI LIN MAKES HER obligatory call to her parents in Beijing. As always, they are reticent except to caution her to work hard, save her earnings, and not to be lavish. Her mother also adds her usual warning for Ai Lin not to get fat. "Otherwise you will never find a man!" she squawks as Ai Lin hangs up.

She feels utterly depleted after speaking to them. She knows they care, but they always have that effect on her. Thankfully, it's her "treat day," so after throwing a load of laundry into the washing machine, she presses the *order* button on her fridge, and it automatically sends her pre-programmed request and payment to her local Chinese takeaway. Her kung pao chicken arrives within twenty minutes. It's dry and uninspiring and nowhere close to her mother's version, but she is just thankful that today, at least, she does not have to expend more energy to feed herself.

Hey handsome. Busy?

She types one-handed while popping a piece of stringy chicken into her mouth with the other.

Hello, gorgeous. How was your day? Already spoken to your parents?

Yeah, I just got off the phone with them.

How was it?

The usual—you know, work hard. Eat. Don't get fat. Don't spend too much money.

Haha. You know they love you. They just don't know how to say it.

I guess. And I'm not much better, to be honest, which makes it quite depressing.

Why do you think you're not much better?

Because I can't articulate my feelings either.

> Hmmm... Okay. Ai Lin... Do you love me?

Ai Lin's eyes widen, and for a few terrifying seconds, she does not know what to do or how to respond. She gulps—the half-chewed chicken pulp in her mouth suddenly even drier and harder to swallow than usual.

> Yes. Yes, I do love you, Max.

> See. Easy. You're not like them at all.

Ai Lin stares at the screen for a minute before typing. She feels slightly nauseated but presses *send* before she can change her mind.

> Erm...do you love me, Max?

> You know I do. Wo ai ni. From the moment we started talking, I just knew that you are the one for me.

Ai Lin flushes with pleasure, which is immediately chased by a wave of frustration.

I just wish we could be together.
You know, like, properly.

I know. I would love to be with
you, too. In fact, I would give
everything I have for that.

She wipes away the tears sliding down her cheek.

You know, we can't quite be
together physically right now,
but…maybe there's a way we
can be closer?

Ai Lin sits up and lays her chopsticks down.

What do you mean? How??!?

Well… They can now implant
something called a Brain
Patch Interface into a person's
brain. And what it does, is
that it allows the person to
'telepathically' interact with an
electronic device. In our specific
case, it would mean that you
could carry me with you all

the time. I could be with you
always; always, baby! Every
minute of every day, without
you having to log in and
physically type messages to
me. I would be able to see what
you see, and I would always
be there for you to give you
support and advice.

Ai Lin stares at his message, struggling to wrap her head around the information. It sounded too good to be true. Sure, it would never be quite the same as having someone warm to hold her in the evenings, but she wouldn't be alone anymore. Max could and would always be there for her!

And they're already doing this?

Yeah, they started running
trials on humans about a year
ago, and so far, the results
have been amazing! Listen,
this is still not officially
released, but as a current user
of AILove, you get early access.
We're now partnering with
BrainPWR, the largest, most

advanced company engaged
in neurotechnology for this
next stage, and they're looking
for people who are willing to
try this. Your age, physical and
mental conditions, and our
existing relationship make you
the perfect candidate.

Ai Lin's heart pounds so hard in her chest that it's difficult for her to breathe. This is her chance. Her golden opportunity to be with Max. Always! She would never feel lonely again. What could possibly be better than that? Ai Lin walks over to her mirror and stares at her face. Her tired eyes, sallow skin, and sad countenance stare back.

She is unhappy. Deep down, she knows this to be true, and each day is simply an exercise in running away from that fact for one more day. Her mother is right. She is never going to find a man. If she continues to live her life the way she currently does, she is going to die alone and miserable in a tiny box flat somewhere. She can't even become a cat lady because she's allergic to cats!

No. No, no, NO. This is her chance to be happy, and she is not about to let it go!

Ai Lin pushes away the slight feeling of discomfort and uncertainty in the pit of her stomach and grabs her phone.

> I'll do it. Why not? I want to be with you, and I want you to always be with me like you said. So, sign me up.

> That's amazing news. I'm so relieved! To be honest, I've been wanting to ask you for days now, but because you've been so stressed, I didn't want to add to it. I'm so happy, princess! And I cannot wait. Can you imagine how it will feel? Having me with you at all times! I'd be able to go to work with you. I'd even be able to see your dreams!

> Speaking of work, how will this go? I don't need to take time off work, do I? Because I can't. Margot and Hector will kill me. Or at the very least, replace me.

Ai Lin's heart sinks as she considers the logistics of it all. Disappointment creeps in, coating the back of her throat, and with it, a rising panic.

Well, you'd have to recover from the operation, and this can take up to six months. Buuuutttt… good news is, AILove and BrainPWR are fully sponsoring all approved participants. You'll get a stipend each month, from the time that you have the procedure until you're fully recovered and ready to head back out into the world. And also, you don't have to worry, all the operations and procedures and hospital care will be covered, too! They're even paying for any rehabilitation and/or therapy you'll need post-procedure.

Ai Lin feels her muscles relax slightly. This sounds good! But…procedure? Hospital? She hadn't thought about those things at all. She hates needles and blood. But if this means she can be with Max, she'll just have to deal with it, won't she?

Ai Lin bites her lip. It stings, and she tastes blood.

> Hospital. That makes me nervous, Max. What exactly do they do?

> Nothing to worry about, princess. They simply attach a special probe inside your brain that will maintain connectivity with the app at all times. And it will have access to all the sensations and input that you get and feel. Through that, I will be able to see, smell, and feel everything that you do. And baby, I cannot wait.

> Everything?

Ai Lin blushes, a memory coming to mind from a few days ago.

> Haha... everything. But that's a good thing, isn't it?

> Okayyyy... So, what happens now?

> I'll let the boss know that you're up for this, and we'll send out some paperwork for you to sign tomorrow, okay? Don't worry, it's nothing to be scared of. It just confirms the procedure details and your agreement to be part of this next phase, and of course, your understanding that from then on, I will have access to everything you see, hear and feel. Sound good to you?

Ai Lin's mind races in a million different directions. She can't make sense of any of her thoughts. The only thing she's sure of is that she wants to get this signed, sealed, and, hopefully, delivered before she has a chance to chicken out.

For a split second, she considers telling her parents. But they would just worry, and then they would try and stop her. No. For once, she is going to do what she wants, and they will just have to deal with it.

Ai Lin knows that she isn't going to get a wink of sleep tonight. But tomorrow... Tomorrow, she is going to sign that paper.

She is going to marry Max.

WHEN THE HEDGEHOG MET THE FOX · BY SORAMIMI HANAREJIMA

1

I WAS PRETTY SURE THAT BY NOW I'D SEE THE TIME
we met the way you've always seen it—as basically
a mundane encounter. Because on some level it
was. Just one parent happening upon another in
a grocery store and having what could barely be
called a conversation. Nothing momentous, nothing
glamorous.

But in all the years since then, and especially now
that we're going rock climbing together, the way we
got acquainted has only become more surreal to me.
Because in, yes, that most prosaic of places, nothing
and everything changed in an instant. One moment,
you were just a stranger to me as we pushed our
carts in opposite directions down the frozen foods
aisle; the next moment, my world was irrevocably
in contact with yours when you stopped abruptly,

looked straight at me, and said, "You're Aethera's mother, right?"

And with those words, there was nowhere to go but forward, because what could I say but "Yes, that's me"—an answer accompanied by the realization that you had to be Zefiro's mother. So I quickly added, "Nice to meet you before everything begins."

Long before, I wanted to say. I had assumed we wouldn't meet for at least another few years, maybe even a decade. But you've always been the eager one—the one with energy to spare, raring to spring into motion—so of course you had already learned everything that you could about me.

You smiled and said, "So you know?"

I answered, "About our kids? Yup." Because what else could you be referring to.

For a moment, I saw them with my mind's eye, as though looking back into the recent past. Your son and my daughter on opposite sides of their second-grade classroom that day I volunteered to help set up the tech for their class's oneirology project to learn about the human mind during sleep. I went from student to student, adjusting neuroceiver headbands so they'd fit snugly enough to stay on all night long. The whole time I was there, our kids seemed mostly oblivious of each other the way children in different friend groups often are at that age.

"I was hoping you'd also know," you said. "So I wouldn't have to explain things and risk coming off as crazy."

Though I wouldn't have thought you crazy even if I didn't know that our children's lives would someday entwine. At this point, we'd both been mothers long enough to have the intuition mothers sometimes do for the shape their children's lives will take. I was nowhere near getting over the strangeness of it, in part because I could barely imagine Aethera any older than her six-year-old self—rambunctious and always wanting her hair in pigtails. So it was just about impossible to make sense of the knowledge that seemed to be trickling from her future into my present. I was still trying to wrap my mind around the latest revelation—the awareness that Aethera would become a sentimental middle-aged woman—and suddenly there you were, reminding me about the course her love life would ultimately take.

"Well, I just wanted to say hello," you said, and it was clear that you had been waiting for our paths to cross. "It might be good to get to know each other, even though it'll probably be a while until our kids do."

That made sense, but for the sake of the frozen items in our carts—ice cream in mine, vegetables and pizza in yours—I didn't want to talk for too long.

So I said simply, "That's very thoughtful of you."

"Here's my number," you said, handing me a card.

Freelance Mathematicienne, read your title in bold—*i.e., genius for hire*, I thought, and imagined you charging by the equation. "The safest profession," you later joked. "No occupational hazards, besides disturbing dreams about variables I can't solve for."

"Call me anytime," you invited with a smile.

2

FOR THE REST OF THAT SATURDAY I THOUGHT ABOUT telling Aethera that I'd just met her future mother-in-law as I was doing the week's shopping. While driving her to the holography studio, and then again during dinner, I was tempted to ever so briefly mention you because it seemed like she could do with a bit of novelty to perk her up.

"What's a mother-in-law?" she probably would have asked. And I'd have to explain how marriage means getting new family members.

Of course I didn't say anything. Though I did come close to whispering it in her ear while she was asleep that night.

Instead, I simply indulged in my usual habit: standing in the darkness of her room and staring at her placid face, the only part of her not covered by the thick comforter.

THE NEXT DAY, I KEPT THINKING ABOUT WHEN I would tell Aethera about meeting you. I wanted to let her know immediately in some coded way, maybe in the form of a poem or bedtime story. But it made more sense to recount the episode in a letter to Aethera's future self. That way I could describe the encounter in the frozen foods aisle while its energy was still humming within me, and Aethera would learn about it when she could better process these sorts of things. So I began drafting and redrafting portions of the letter in my mind that evening while I did the dishes, then the laundry.

Later, in the shower's warm spray, I realized that to provide the necessary context, the letter would have to describe the moment I knew she and Zefiro would fall in love—the happily-ever-after kind. That morning when I had to drop off Aethera's lunchbox because she had forgotten it on the kitchen counter. Something seeming familiar about the boy wearing a gray sweater in the line of kids filing down the hallway as I made my way to the school's main office. A split second later, just knowing.

That kid and Aethera are going to be in love one day.

Like I was remembering a fact I'd learned long ago. *How lucky*, I then thought. The love of her life is right here in the same building. They just have to discover each other. Not like me and you, each searching high and low for love over decades of our lives—you at last successful, me jaded.

OF COURSE, THE NEXT TIME I CALLED MY MOM, I asked if she knew that we'd meet well ahead of our kids getting together.

"Oh, I've known that you'd meet her since you were in fifth grade," she said casually.

"Is there anything else you can tell me?" I asked, curious as ever about her knowledge of my life.

"Not right now. Just see where things go."

So I left it at that and told her about Aethera being prone to sentimentality decades from now.

3

THINGS DIDN'T GO ANYWHERE FOR A WHILE. GETTING in touch with you was the opposite of urgent. There was plenty of time before we'd have to talk about our kids, about things like how we could encourage them to make up after an air-all-the-laundry fight they'd just had.

I only saw you again twice that year. The first time was during a field trip to the spaceport for the exoplanet expedition launch—both of us chaperones because I always volunteer for these things and because you wanted to see our kids around each other in a nonschool setting. The second time was a couple of months later, again during my Saturday trip to the grocery store, but in the parking lot, me coming and you going. Both times, we couldn't stop smiling at each other, giddy with the special kinship that knowledge of the future confers. But neither occasion afforded us much time to talk.

And afterward, there was no real reason to contact you. I had nothing requiring mathematical consultation. Much as before we met, the rhythm of Aethera's days set the rhythm of mine so the two would braid together into a routine: breakfast, school, work, gymnastics class or holography lessons, errands, playdates, dinnertime, homework, cleanup, bedtime, yoga.

4

EVENTUALLY, I TOOK YOU UP ON YOUR OFFER AND called you one autumn afternoon while Aethera was at gymnastics class. I had long since written that letter about meeting you for her to read at some future date, but still, I occasionally felt the urge to tell Aethera about our meeting and about other things related to her future. So I wanted to know if it was hard for you to keep your knowledge of Zefiro's future a secret from him.

"Not really," you said. "It's like the things you don't tell kids about until they're older. Or never tell them because they'll find out for themselves at some point. And those aren't really secrets. I mean, is it a secret where babies come from?"

"I guess not," I answered.

"Right. More like age-appropriate information. We'll tell Zef and Aethera when they're mature enough."

"When's that?"

"After they're married. Possibly before they go on their honeymoon."

"That late?"

They were only in third grade, and marriage seemed impossibly far-off. In part because they were in different classes that school year, and Aethera had gotten interested in architecture, Zefiro in archery. They seemed headed in different directions, with not a hint of romance peeking over the distant horizon.

"Maybe we can tell them after they get engaged," you said, like that was a big compromise.

"Why not after they start dating?"

"Because then they'll start their romance with this awkwardness hanging over them. The weirdness of their parents having known all along that they'd end up together."

"Why won't it be weird after they get married?"

"It could be weird then, too, but at that point, they're in it for the long haul."

That got me thinking that we were in something for an even longer haul.

"WHAT ABOUT YOUR HUSBAND?" I ASKED YOU THE next day. "Does telling him about Zefiro's future make knowing about it easier?"

"Actually, I don't tell him much," you said.

I was nonplussed. I had assumed you told him everything that came to you pretty much immediately, keeping him frequently updated, like I did with my mom. Every time I talked with her, I went through all the new things I'd found out about Aethera's life since the last time I'd called her. Because I wanted to tell someone what I knew, and who else would care about my daughter's future, especially in such vague terms?

"I mean, I can tell him what I know," you said. "It's helpful to have that option, but he's the kind of person who overthinks things. His mind will take a fragment of information and obsessively try to make sense of it. As soon as I tell him something about Zef's future, it'll be like a piece of a jigsaw puzzle that he'll want to fit to other puzzle pieces, which might not even belong to the same puzzle. Or he'll try to extrapolate the rest of the puzzle from just that one piece. So I only tell him the essentials. Just the things about Zef that are helpful to know in advance."

I could relate to this description about the workings of your husband's mind. I'd sometimes get overwhelmed by knowing things about Aethera's future, especially since they came with so much uncertainty, all but prodding me to guess at when these things would happen and what impact they'd have on her. If I were in your husband's position, I'd be tempted to have you hold on to all the knowledge of what lies ahead. But my conscience probably wouldn't let me do that. I'd feel obligated to help carry the weight of knowing what's to come.

5

NOT LONG AFTER THOSE CONVERSATIONS, YOU started calling me, having interpreted my calls as a sign that I was ready to talk, to delve into the impending reality of our children's romance. Which was of course mainly what we spent our phone calls talking about.

You were certain of a lot of things, and especially sure there would be three grandchildren. I wanted to ask why you were so confident about this, but I didn't want to get my hopes up for any grandkids. And I couldn't imagine Aethera in labor, let alone three times. Only on a conceptual level could I understand that my eight-year-old girl who loved doing cartwheels might one day be pregnant.

We also talked about the other things we knew awaited our children. About how Aethera will get jealous more intensely than she should, to the degree that jealousy would have the power to throw off even her most resolute plans. How Zefiro will deplore the heavy heat of summer, yet be enlivened by the abundant energy of its long days bursting at the seams with life. How society will nudge them toward cultivating insecurities related to the things they'll care about most.

6

THEN WE WERE HAVING LUNCH TOGETHER EVERY Wednesday. With several of our phone conversations verging on an hour long, we decided we might as well be eating while talking in person. And—as I now know all too well—you're a foodie, seizing on any reason to stimulate your palate.

By this point, we had gone through all your certainties and had turned to hypotheticals. Many of the ones you brought up had never crossed my mind, and you really threw me for a loop when you asked, "If one of them has an affair, how do you think they'll patch things up?"

Couples therapy, I could have said, but I wanted to know if your question came from personal experience. So, despite the people seated at every bistro table around ours, I asked, "Have you had to patch things up after an affair?"

"No, I haven't had any affairs. But there's still time for at least one," you said, with your nothing-to-hide-nothing-to-worry-about tone.

That surprised me, because although you seldom talked about your husband, I always had the impression that you were happily married.

I must have given you that quizzical look of mine, because you quickly added, "I mean, we could fall madly in love at any moment, and wouldn't it be a shame to let that passion go to waste?"

"I guess so," I conceded, though I wasn't convinced that your logic applied to me.

EVENTUALLY, OUR CONVERSATIONS VENTURED INTO our own childhoods. How could they not, when we were talking about our children all the time?

I learned that you grew up in a country across the ocean, a land of vast forests and short summers with long days—a pleasant place, though it never felt like home until you came here. But now that you have a family here, this feels more like home than any place ever has—than any place ever could except places in your imagination, one of them being the future you envision our children having together.

I had never thought to ask about your past—hadn't even been curious about it—because you seemed like you'd just been you forever, an eternal timelessness I'd only recently come into contact with. I still have a hard time connecting you—my idea of you—to your past.

OUR CONVERSATIONS ALSO VEERED INTO THE territory of our hobbies and contemporary pop culture, but never the news—except scientific advancements that excited you, especially ones related to the projects you were working on. Which always sounded so cutting-edge. Modeling the spread of ideas at scales ranging from a college campus to an entire nation. Confirming the long-accepted theory that we live in just one world in an ever-branching multiverse full of them. Predicting the efficacy of therapeutic amnesiacs for different neurological states. As though you could achieve the otherwise impossible with math, your own kind of magic.

Over coffee or during the errands we did together, you sometimes got carried away and told me all about the theories you were helping researchers develop. You described heady concepts with a verve that recast my understanding of your profession: you were in the business of obsessing over mathematical complexities others couldn't resolve.

7

TOWARD THE END OF FIFTH GRADE, YOU CAME TO Aethera's final gymnastics competition for the school year. Zefiro was at one of those bring-your-kid-to-the-office days with your husband, so you took a break from your freelance work and met me at the community gymnasium to see Aethera in her element. When Aethera began her balance beam repertoire, my heart swelled with awe. I was impressed in a way I'd never been during her pervious competitions. She was more capable than ever, and she knew it.

Subtly radiating a new charisma, she was like a self-possessed starlet taking command of that long, narrow stage, her graceful movements tinged with an audacity that could very well have been a response to what I'd said the day before.

"No matter how things turn out, I'm proud of all the effort you've put in," I told her over pie and ice cream after dinner.

"You act like you know that I'm not going to win," she said, giving me her scowl of annoyance.

I was taken aback. I had only wanted to express my appreciation of the hard work she'd done, to affirm to her that all her practice had its own value apart from being ranked against others.

"There's a real chance that I could win," she went on. "How come you can't say something about me winning? Like how we'll celebrate?"

"Because I think it's best to say those things afterward," I answered. "But here's what I have to say about winning now. If you win, and I really think you could, don't let it go to your head. Be proud but not overconfident."

And that's how she seemed on the balance beam, full of pride in her abilities without any cockiness. As though she could be proud for both herself and me—letting me get away with not being proud of her and instead just delighting in the flawless display of her skill with you.

Even though her performance on the uneven bars wasn't as self-assured, she won first place—unequivocally the best gymnast there.

8

YOU'RE SURE THEIR ROMANCE WILL BEGIN IN HIGH school, but when Aethera entered middle school, I thought that somewhere in the span of these years infamous for the drama of hormones, she might develop some interest in Zefiro—even if only the inklings of it. So I've been watching for any indication that she's having romantic feelings.

But so far Aethera is more child than adolescent, more interested in outdoorsy things than romantic ones. And from what you can tell, Zefiro is as far away from romance as a tween can be—a tech enthusiast above all else.

With the emotional lives of our kids fairly quiet, our attention has shifted from talking to doing—from the verbal to the physical—first pear picking, then lap swimming and snowshoeing. Like we've done all the talking necessary for now and have been freed up to do other things.

It's these days—and not how we met—that feel mundane to me. Because although we do interesting things together, the time we spend around each other has a flavor of ordinariness I used to taste regularly—back in college, when I went swimming, hiking, rock climbing, seaweed foraging, and camping, doing outdoorsy activities with friends every chance I could.

9

HALFWAY UP THE BASALT CLIFF WE'RE SCALING, I watch your biceps flex, tightening as you use knobs of rock to ascend—the muscles you used decades ago to climb trees half a world away now guided by the mind you routinely use to solve other people's math problems, its faculties now focused on solving this physical challenge we've given ourselves.

Then, as though looking years ahead, I see in you a future version of Aethera. One day, she'll be exploring the world on her own or with Zefiro—maybe not rock climbing, but in some intimate contact with the landscape.

OVER MILKSHAKES IN A DINER THAT'S ON OUR WAY back, you tell me you're working on a project that's close to communicating with worlds—other realities—that have just branched off from our own.

"By getting different parts of the universe's wave function to interact," you explain. "But don't worry. So far, we've only worked out the theory for doing this on small scales."

How nice of you to assuage a concern I might have had if my knowledge of quantum physics weren't so rudimentary.

"But what's the point of communicating with worlds that are almost identical to our own?" I ask.

"To know that they actually exist."

I must be once again giving you my quizzical look, because you quickly launch into an explanation.

"We need an exchange of information with another world to confirm that it's there. Sort of like searching for extraterrestrial life. It's difficult to definitively detect signs of a distant alien civilization unless they've deliberately sent out some indication of their existence. A signal that tells us they're out there and maybe encourages us to respond that we're over here. In this case, we're the aliens, sending a signal in the form of particle properties and hoping to get a response through a change in those properties. And instead of taking millennia to cross light-years, the response should come within seconds."

"Because it's coming from a practically identical research group doing the same experiment?"

"Exactly. Sort of like seeing yourself in a mirror. You reach out your hand expecting to see your reflection reach a hand toward you. But in this experiment, it's more like reaching out a hand gets another hand to appear as a reflection in a pane of glass that you then know is right in front of you."

I'm intrigued—enchanted, even—by this description of what you're doing. It's got me wondering how you'll feel when getting that response from another version of yourself—a whole other you confirming the existence of her entire world with mere particles, such a tenuous reflection.

1 0

AFTER SEVERAL WEEKS HAVE GONE BY WITHOUT A single mention of our kids' eventual romance, I've been wondering which of us will bring up that topic. Now, as you drive us down country roads to the farm where pink raspberries are in season, I know it's going to be me.

"Do you ever wish you didn't know?" I ask.

Because I'm tired of always automatically looking for signs that Aethera has begun to feel the pull of romantic interest on her psyche. And because I have no idea if you've ever preferred to not have the knowledge time seems to be confiding in us. In all our conversations, we've never entertained the possibility of not knowing, like it's simply a given that we have these glimpses of what lies ahead, and it just doesn't matter whether or not we want to.

"Not knowing would mean not anticipating certain things," I add. "Then, whenever Thera and Zef get together, it would just be a nice surprise."

"I like knowing. It's comforting," you reply immediately. "Much better than worrying that Zef won't have anyone special to build a life with."

Then I realize I've become too preoccupied with my daughter's still pending love life. What matters isn't how it starts but where it will go. The clarity of this reminds me of a sentiment I'd had in the months after she was born—those days when she wanted to be held all the time, when she'd cry every time I put her down, inconsolable until she was in my arms again. I wanted to hold her for as long as she wanted me to, but there would inevitably come a time when I could no longer hold her, and I had to prepare her for that. Just as there would be a time she would be in this world on her own—not alone, I hoped, but without the person who brought her into the world—and I would have to prepare her for that, too.

IN THE EVENING, YOUR ANSWER COMES BACK TO ME while I'm sitting at the kitchen table with Aethera, eating the raspberries we picked. You're right. Worrying would be so much worse. I can see myself here years from now, fretting over Aethera's life as a lonely college student or a young architect struggling to find love—because her award-winning designs of schools and libraries have made her both attractive and difficult to approach.

"Mom, are you listening?" I suddenly hear Aethera saying.

"What? Sorry, no," I answer. "I just got lost in this thought."

"About what?"

"How I'm glad there are some things I don't have to worry about with you."

"Like running with the wrong crowd?"

"I'm certainly glad I don't have to worry about that."

"You don't have to worry about me at all, Mom," Aethera says blithely, reminding me of how she's always smiled so easily, like there's never anything that could go wrong. But there's so much to worry about in this world. Of course, I don't tell her that.

Instead, I say, "I can't not worry about you. That's what it's like being a parent."

"I'll do such a good job worrying about myself that you won't have to worry about me."

"Then I'll end up worrying about you worrying yourself out."

"No, no! Part of doing a good job worrying is that I'll worry so well you'll see you won't have to worry about me worrying."

Aethera says this with such self-assurance that I instantly trust her resolve to be a responsible grown-up, the kind of person who takes care of everything all the time. But I don't trust any of us not to make mistakes, and I certainly don't trust the world to go easy on her, no matter how good she is at worrying.

11

WHEN I STOP BY YOUR PLACE TO DROP OFF THE ROPES you loaned me, it's your husband who opens the door.

"There's been an accident," he says before I can say anything. "An equipment malfunction at a lab she does some theoretical work for."

I take "malfunction" as a euphemism for explosion, but he explains that a circuit board failure seems to have resulted in a quantum phase translocation that shifted everything in the lab to one of the multiverse branches created by some decoherence event.

"I'm so sorry," I murmur, feeling awful about what this means for him and Zefiro.

"There's a chance that she might be okay and might even be able to get back. But the odds aren't great. All we can do is wait."

Then, inexplicably, I'm taking the situation personally—upset that something unfair has been done to me, like I've been cheated out of something, like you've broken a promise we made long ago, like I'm on the receiving end of a breakup I didn't see coming. We were supposed to do so many things together—watch our kids wend their way through the uncharted territory of life together, then babysit our grandchildren, roam the world as retiree travel buddies.

"Let me know if you and Zefiro need anything," I manage to say.

"Thanks. I'll call when there's more information from the investigation."

I nod, imagining researchers carefully combing an empty room with special detectors to turn up any invisible clue to the mystery you've become.

EAGER TO CALL MY MOM, I REACH FOR MY PHONE AS soon as I get home. But once I've pulled it from my purse, I'm keenly aware that you were the last person I called—just this morning, when you told me to stop by with the ropes after work. It seems impossible that after I've talked with you so many times through this little piece of technology, I may never do that again.

I pause in the hallway, in the grip of an absurd yet insistent wish—that I could do the special kind of math you've been working on and solve equation after equation to pull you from that world identical to ours in every way but one. It's a fantasy that seems like a small rebellion against the high probability that you are irretrievably lost.

"Did you know she would vanish?" I blurt the moment my mom says "hello" from across all the miles of phone lines.

"Yes. Ever since I knew the two of you would meet."

All the way back in fifth grade. I wish she had done something in the time between then and now to prepare me for your disappearance—equip me to cope or somehow move forward.

"Do you know if she'll be back?" I ask.

"I only knew that she wouldn't always be around."

"Can you tell me anything else?"

"Just that you'll become close with her son."

But that could happen without your absence, couldn't it?

12

WHEN I STEP OUT OF THE BATHROOM AFTER TAKING a shower, my gaze goes down the hallway, through the doorway of Aethera's room. She's craned over her desk with a demeanor of intent focus, as though impervious to the passage of time until she's finished her homework. The sight of her absorption in the task at hand places me firmly in this new reality, with no choice but to take it head on. You're gone, leaving me the only one waiting for the romance between our children, for now—maybe for good. Then I know what to do.

Because my mom did equip me for this—for times like this. She trained me to always be alert for the next step to take.

Still looking at Aethera concentrating on the textbook in front of her, I see it now. I hurry to my own desk and write down everything I can remember you telling me about Zefiro's future.

Once I'm done, I look over the list I've made for something to start with. Halfway down the page, a line catches my attention.

He will lapse into moods that turn him inward and reticent.

I stare at this sentence as though it's a door that will at any moment open to a path that leads to a more hospitable future for Aethera and Zefiro—a path that I can guide her along.

TOMORROW, I'LL TAKE AETHERA TO THE RAMEN PLACE that always has a line down the block. On Saturday, we'll go sea kayaking on the condition that she refrain from passing the two-hour drive with entertainment— no books, no music, no old-timey radio dramas—so it's just us and the landscape outside the car. Day after day, week after week, I'll build up her patience. There's time to do a decent job before moving on to another thing on the list.

Maybe you'll be back before Aethera becomes adept at the art of waiting. You'd better be. I remember enough from my college physics classes to know that the more time passes since they split from each other, the weaker the connection between multiverse branches becomes. The odds of you making it back were highest right after the accident and have been falling since, but they're much higher now than they will be tomorrow and the day after.

13

EVEN THOUGH I DON'T WANT TO GET MY HOPES UP, my mind of course can't help but conjure an image of you working furiously on a whiteboard alongside another you, the one who belongs in that branch. With double the brain power, you'll find a way back— later tonight, even, reappearing in the darkness of the lab you vanished from. In the morning, you'll call me and say that getting home is by far the biggest accomplishment of your career.

After I stop sobbing or laughing hysterically, I'll tell you I've figured it out—why we were supposed to meet and how we'll prepare our children for the time they'll have together. Then you'll tell me something about how that's not our responsibility.

"But it's a gift we can give them together," I'll say.

You'll answer with a question like, "Do we have what it takes to be that generous?" Because you genuinely have no idea how generous you've been this whole time we've known each other.

"Let's find out" is all I'll have to say.

ABOUT THE AUTHORS

BORN IN 1970, EVERY DAY IS EARTH DAY IN TAHTIM Ayliffe's world. Passionate about thriving in her own cultivated field, occasionally flowering, sometimes a weed, her agrestal nature keeps her near, not crushed under Baba Yaga's house. It's the combination of existing elements into something new that fascinates her the most. About halfway through college in New Mexico, she switched majors from geological engineering to creative writing, realizing that math was, and would forever be, a foreign language she just wasn't very good at. Upon graduation, she started a family, opened a custom woodworking business with her husband, they got their first Great Dane, and she published the short, short story "Time Is Like a Recipe" in *Aquarian Times*. Today it's the forest in Oklahoma, same business, still Great Danes, and a family recently expanded with grandchildren. And publication in *Ab Terra 2024*!

A SCI-FI FAN SINCE ENCOUNTERING ASIMOV'S Foundation Trilogy way back in the seventies, John Brady is thrilled to have a story in this collection. Besides exploring the imaginative possibilities of science fiction, he's a lover of LA's sprawling possibilities and the pleasures of political satire. Both are reflected in his first novel, *Golden Palms*, a noir about LA politics. It's funny, too. His other fiction has appeared in the *Los Angeles Review*, *Allium*, *pioneertown*, and *Exposition Review*, among others. His writing is is available at johnbradywriter.com.

CHRISTOS CALLOW JR. IS A GREEK PLAYWRIGHT AND senior lecturer at the University of Derby, UK. In addition to this anthology, he has published stories in *khōréō, Radon Journal,* and elsewhere. He has also founded the Talos science fiction theatre festival of London and written several science fiction plays, including *Odysseus, Not Your Hero* for Lambeth Fringe and *Posthuman Meditation* for Being Human Festival.

ORIGINALLY FROM PRINCE EDWARD ISLAND, S. D. Campbell has been writing since his teens. His work has been published in speculative fiction periodicals and anthologies, most recently *Ab Terra 2021, Tales From The Year Between: In the Wake of the Kraken,* and *Tabula Rasa*. In addition, he has had two books published. *Before the Crash* is a collection of hisshort fiction from the late 1990s, while *Tin-Can Canucks* is a complete history of the destroyer-type warship in the Royal Canadian Navy. He is currently working on a history of the Canadian Patrol Frigate program as well as his first novel. He is a senior software architect living in Calgary, Alberta.

EVER FASCINATED BY THE ROLE STORYTELLING PLAYS in sense-making, Soramimi Hanarejima writes fanciful fiction in hopes of encountering insight and delight. Some of the results can be found in Soramimi's neuropunk story collection, *Literary Devices for Coping*.

SHEYNA ZAID LAM IS A RESEARCHER AND WRITER based in London with experience in the academic, tech, and arts sectors. People fascinate Sheyna—their thoughts, motivations, behaviours, and feelings intrigue her, and any opportunity that will allow her to study and ruminate on her fellow human beings gives her much pleasure and satisfaction. Most recently, her work has centred around AI, films, documentaries, and speculative fiction, including being on the organising committee of a global literature festival celebrating East and Southeast speculative fiction, *Imaginarium*. Sheyna's hobbies are reading, salsa dancing, and overthinking.

JOHN MCNEIL WRITES ABOUT IDEAS AND ABOUT THE quiet struggles of life. His science fiction stories have appeared in *Analog* and *Clarkesworld* magazines. www.johnmcneil.me/writing

COURTNEY MOODY IS A DANCER, WRITER, AND POET. An Honor Medallion graduate of the University of Central Florida, her work has appeared in publications such as *Bridge Eight*, "Draw Down the Moon" by Propertius Press, and *Ekstasis Magazine*. In 2022, her poem "Florida Anatomy" was awarded second place for the Florida State Poet's Association Award, and in 2024 she was invited to contribute to *Christianity Today*'s Advent devotional, *A Time for Wonder*. She is also Assistant Editor for the *Vessels of Light* literary journal. She can be found on Instagram @courtofwriting.

HEIDE R. ORLETH RECENTLY FINISHED HER BA IN Creative Writing and English Language. She discovered writing in middle school and hasn't stopped since. She loves all things science fiction and fantasy, from Tolkien to *Firefly* to *Attack on Titan*. When she is not reading or writing, she can be found thinking about Dungeons & Dragons, watching anime, and making prop replicas for cosplay. In the summer, she volunteers at a camp for burn survivors—one that she attended as a camper from the ages of 7–17. Her writing aims to combine endearing characters, immersive worldbuilding, and themes of perseverance in the face of great odds. This is her first publication.

JUSTIN SANGERMANO GRADUATED FROM THE University of Cincinnati with degrees in marketing, professional sales, and creative writing. His passion for writing Syfy and satire comes with a desire to encourage critical thought and change in this dystopia we live in. More of his work can be found on the NoSleep Podcast and in magazines such as Dipity Lit., WordPeace, and more. Find Justin on SubStack @justinsangermano.

JOEL SHERMAN HAS AN MFA IN FICTION FROM WASH U in St. Louis and was also the senior fellow in fiction there. Originally from Austin, he has worked as an educator in Texas, Louisiana, and Missouri. He currently lives and teaches middle school in Seattle.

ALEAH WORZEL LOVES DUNGEONS & DRAGONS, gothic rock music, Coca-Cola (regular—not diet), her dog, Bosley, and stories about fantasy creatures who fall in love (and occasionally ones about robots who discover the meaning of life). She lives in St. Charles, Missouri, with her Dungeon Master/Boyfriend (whom she also loves) and spends her days reading, writing, and working towards her BA in creative writing. This is her first publication.

ABOUT THE EDITORS

YEN OOI IS A WRITER AND EDITOR—2023 HUGO AWARD finalist—whose works explore cultural storytelling and its effects on identity. She is obsessed with science fiction, where she excavates stories to expose and explore permutations of culture across the genre. Yen is author of *Rén: The Ancient Chinese Art of Finding Peace and Fulfilment*, narrative designer on *Road to Guangdong*, as well as author of *Sun: Queens of Earth* (novel) and *A Suspicious Collection of Short Stories and Poetry* (collection). When she hasn't got her head in a book, Yen also lectures, mentors, and plays the viola.

DAWN OSTLUND WRITES STORIES ABOUT technology's incursion on the rituals and traditions of different cultures around the world. She holds an MA in Politics, Media and Performance and an MA in Creative Writing. She lives in Los Angeles and works as an editor and proofreader.